You NEVER KNOW What YOU'RE GOING TO GET

An Anthology of Short Stories

Edited by
Juleus Ghunta

chalkboard 🍁
publishing

Cover art © 2025 Chalkboard Publishing Inc
Cover art by Anil N. Singh
Edited by Juleus Ghunta
ISBN: 9781771058933

Printed in Canada

This project is funded in part by the Government of Canada

Canada

Contents

Finding Mimi

by Jaimie Franchi

Everyone is afraid of Mimi. Everyone except me. Mimi lives in the woods, and she's not scary. I've never met her, but I've heard enough to know. She's different, and you might say she's weird, but I think everyone is a little weird. I know I am. At every sleepover, there's a Mimi story: about how she lets chickens in her house, traps hunters and eats them, or howls during full moons. I don't think Mimi eats hunters. I think she's probably vegetarian.

Everyone in my town is the same. They all listen to the same music, watch the same shows, wear the same clothes. I never see anyone different, and the only people I hear about who are different are characters in books—and Mimi.

I've never told a Mimi story, but I've never stood up for her either. No one knows how I feel about her. No one knows much about me at all. I'm loud on the inside but quiet on the outside.

Since I'm quiet, I get lonely. Sometimes kids are mean to me. This morning, my neighbour Bernie ran past me yelling, "Moon Girl, Moon Girl!" It sounds cool, but he doesn't mean it in a cool way. He means I daydream, especially in school, and for some reason, everyone points it out.

I don't always stick up for myself, but today, Bernie pushed me too far. It was the third time this week from him, and that's too much.

"Shut up! SHUT UP!" I surprised even myself. Bernie walked toward me.

"Did you just tell me to shut up? OK, weirdo. All you do is daydream and wear weird clothes. When we grow up, it's gonna be you living in the woods instead of that Mimi lady." He laughed, proud of the new insult he invented.

But comparing me to Mimi was a compliment—I was sure of it. He made me more serious about my secret goal: to find Mimi and see her for myself.

Tuesday after school, I walked slowly behind everyone. My brother yelled for me to hurry, but I said I was tired and would catch up.

I left the school path, the one my parents and grandparents took to the same school, all of us walking the same route day in and day out for generations. Without looking back, I headed for the woods.

Everything was scary. I thought I saw someone behind a tree. Was that wrinkly bark a witch's cape? I panicked. I'd been in the woods a million times before, but never alone. I tried to calm down, but I was only ten.

When I found my way back to the school path, my brother was waiting for me.

"What were you doing?!" Sam yelled. He dragged me down the road, mad that he'd missed the pick-up soccer game.

A few weeks later, I was ready to look for Mimi again, but not alone. I needed a partner, and I knew who to ask.

A new family had moved in. Everyone knows everyone in a small town, so new people are big news. The McNichols showed up one Friday with a truck full of overflowing boxes and a van full of kids, all of them messy and loud, except one. The last to climb out of the van was a red-haired girl in a dinosaur t-shirt and sparkly purple skirt, torn and old-looking, like maybe a sister had owned it first.

When I saw her, I knew that Freya and I would be friends. The first minutes were awkward, a lot of "So...what's your favorite book?" and "Do you have any pets?" But after a week, we were playing almost every day.

I told Freya about Mimi, though I knew she'd have heard about her anyway. Mimi had been spotted by a neighbor collecting branches for kindling. She was in overalls and bare feet, feeding deer from her hand, tame as pet dogs. By the next day, everyone knew. I liked the story but hated how everyone made her sound scary. "She's a witch—how else would she get deer to eat out of her hands?" "She's giving them some kind of chemical to tame them." "She's so close to an animal herself that the deer aren't scared." Their imaginations were so small.

When I told Freya my Mimi stories, I made her brave and interesting.

We started something the other kids couldn't know about. We took turns pretending we were Mimi. It's not that we wouldn't have let them play. We knew they'd think we were weird. I didn't need them to have more reasons to tease me.

One day, we got really into the Mimi game. We were in a corner of the playground where no one goes, except us or boys who wanted to fight in private. I pretended to be Mimi, and Freya a fairy who was helping me prepare for a party to celebrate a baby deer. We built a stage with sticks and decorated it with leaves and dandelions.

I was supposed to walk on stage and congratulate the deer mamas and sing a song we had made up. It started off really cool: I walked under the dandelion chain and cleared my throat like I'd seen adults do before making speeches. "We are gathered here to celebrate the birth of our new fawn!" I belted out the song like I was onstage at a concert.

Halfway through the second line, I heard snorting laughs from the bushes. Bernie and his friends, the meanest kids in fourth grade, jumped out. "Bravo, Moon Girl! Nice song, weirdo!" My cheeks were on fire. I wanted to run home. How did they sneak in there without us noticing?

I needed something fun to distract me from Bernie and his gang, so I decided to ask Freya to come find Mimi. I worried she might say no. A few days later, we were alone on the playground. "Let's find Mimi" I half-whispered, half-screeched. I held my breath, as if even the tiniest sound might sway her in the wrong direction.

"Maybe after school tomorrow?" Freya was into it.

The last hour of school took forever. We dawdled from the playground to the walking path, stopping to pretend to tie shoelaces or pick up rocks. My brother ran to the pick-up soccer game, and when he was out of sight, I stopped. "This way," I said, pointing to the barely visible path at the edge of the woods.

For a few minutes, we heard yelling from other kids, arguments about who would play goalie in the soccer game, whose turn it was to wash dishes that night, and whose dress was the prettiest. They were things unimportant to people on a real adventure.

The path rounded a corner, and the shouts faded. The deeper part of the forest opened up and welcomed us. It felt like a fairy tale, with warm winds, chirping birds, and the smells of mud and fallen leaves.

"What if she's not home?" Freya asked. I hadn't thought of that.

"I'm sure she's home. My brother says she hasn't left the forest in ten years. Anyway, we're this far and nothing bad is happening."

The path wasn't very clear, and my legs got tired as we climbed a steep hill. Somehow, it felt like the right direction. I was sweaty and losing my breath and about to give up when we made it to the top.

In the distance stood the most magical home I had ever seen—a crumbling, ivy-covered castle, just like the ones in the fairy tale book in our classroom. We stared until a thunderclap rumbled. I looked at my watch. It was late.

"It's time to go home."

Freya agreed. Though we were a little upset to turn around, we were more excited by our discovery of a whole new world.

"Did you have fun playing with Freya after school?" Mom asked.

I mumbled something about chipmunks and mosquitos. I felt uncomfortable while walking home. I had never lied to Mama before. But I had never told her about my big plan to meet Mimi; I was worried she'd say no.

At home, my stomach hurt, and I wanted to go to bed. I told Mama I didn't feel good and asked to skip dinner. She felt my forehead. "You're not warm. Go lay down, and I'll check on you later." I got into bed and tried to read, but I couldn't concentrate.

"How are you doing, peanut?" Mama asked when she came in later.

"I don't know," I said.

"Is there something you want to tell me?" How do mamas always know?

"I'm worried you'll be mad," I said. Mama promised she wouldn't be mad and said she wanted to make sure I was OK.

"We went...I wanted to tell you...it was fun...nothing bad happened." I couldn't make the words come out right.

"Relax," said Mama. "I'll get you some water. I knew something was wrong." She left and came back with water and ice in my favorite glass.

"We didn't play at the park," I said, my voice scratchy and thin. "Oh? Did something happen?" Mama asked. "Well... we had a plan." I started the story small and quiet, but I got excited about Mimi and the castle and told her everything.

I don't know what I expected her to do, but smiling and giving me her twinkly eyes was not it.

"Daphne," Mama said, "Why didn't you tell me?"

"I don't know. I thought you wouldn't let me. I know what I did was bad." Would she forgive me?

"I'm upset that you didn't tell me. It's my job to keep you safe. Promise me you won't keep things like this from me," she said. "And you're lucky that I know Mimi's castle is safe."

"What do you mean?" I asked.

9

"Daphne, there are many stories I've told you about my childhood," said Mama.

"Yeah," I said, "like when you fell into the pond at your grandpa's house!"

"Yes," said Mama, "like that. There are more, some that I've been saving until you were older, like about how I've known Mimi since I was very young." My jaw dropped.

When Mama was little, her family lived in a log cabin with an outhouse. They had a garden and chickens and a cow. Their front door faced the road, but their backyard was woods. Life was wild but also fun. They cut their Christmas trees from the forest, caught minnows in the stream, built forts in trees, and played hide and seek among the ferns. I've heard some of the stories so often I can tell them myself.

"When I was a kid, the stories about Mimi were tamer. A hundred and fifty years ago, her family, who were kind but rather mysterious, built that castle deep in the woods. For a long time, many townspeople didn't know they were there, and they could have privacy and live as they liked."

"As a child, Grandpapa sometimes worked for her parents, chopping firewood and doing other jobs to earn money. Grandpapa's family was poor. Mimi's family was kind and gracious and found work for him whenever he needed money."

"Mimi's family and the villagers lived peacefully. Things only changed when she started living alone. As the town grew, more trees were cut down and more roads were built. Most of her family left, either to move elsewhere, or because they got old and died, or because they weren't interested in rural life anymore. When her mother died and her sister moved away, Mimi, the youngest sister, an artist, stayed to care for the castle and live in privacy."

"An artist?" Mimi was getting more exciting by the minute.

"As a kid, I knew the stories about Mimi were wrong. I fed her ducks and helped her plant seeds. For Christmas, she baked glittery cookies. In spring, she knew where to find robins' nests with pretty blue eggs. Mimi's house was always lovely."

"Mama," I asked, "why don't you still know Mimi?"

"That's a good question," said Mama, "but I'm not sure I have a good answer. I didn't stop seeing Mimi on purpose. It just happened. I grew up, started babysitting and spending more time with my friends. I went to university, met your dad, and started my adult life down here in town."

"Could you visit her again, Mama? Can we go together?" I begged.

"It's a lovely idea," said Mama. "I've thought about Mimi over the years. I don't know if she wants me to visit her."

"Mama, I'm sure she does! Can we please, please go?" This was my chance.

"I'll take you to visit Mimi if you promise you won't keep something like this from me again," said Mama, in her most serious voice.

"I promise!" I could hardly wait.

On the day of the visit, Freya and I met Mama after school. Bernie was yelling some dumb insult after me, but I was too excited to care.

We headed into the woods and climbed the hill. When we saw the castle, Freya and I started running, but it was further away than it looked. After several minutes, we stopped and dropped our backpacks.

Mama caught up with us, and I realized I was starving. We had forgotten to eat our after-school snack. Mama took pumpkin muffins and trail mix from her backpack.

We inhaled our food, not noticing the person moving deer-like behind us. When she was a few feet away, we finally saw her.

I jumped in shock, and Freya stared, her jaw hanging open. "Hello ladies! I didn't mean to scare you. I've just finished collecting wildflowers. Your mama told me you'd be coming. I'm Mimi. I live in that castle. What are your names?" As if Mimi needed any introduction!

Mama introduced us while we stared precisely the way Mama always told me not to. "This is my daughter Daphne, whom I told you about, and this is her friend Freya. They've been dying to come up here and meet you and see the castle."

"It's nice to meet you," Mimi said. "I see things down in the village sometimes, especially in winter when the trees are bare, but I don't often meet its people; it's rare indeed, so this is special for me. I need to put these flowers in water before they droop. Do you want to come back with me for a little tour?"

A tour. Of Mimi's castle. Given by Mimi. Could this day possibly get any better?

I wasn't sure how Mama wanted me to respond, so I stood silently, staring. Maybe Bernie was right. Maybe I was a weirdo.

"Thank you, Mimi. That sounds wonderful!" Mama replied.

"Perfect!" said Mimi. Then she was off, as swiftly as she had appeared.

We packed up and followed her. I snuck glances at Mama and Freya.

Mama's twinkle-eyed look was back, and Freya did a funny little jump.

Mimi was close to my grandma's age, but she walked as fast as my gym teacher when she leads our class out to the track.

"This is my chicken coop. Over there is my pond. Behind it are my gardens. They need a good weeding, but that's normal for this time of year."

It was like nothing I'd ever seen; a garden, yes, but somehow better, wilder, freer, more magical. I'd never seen land like Mimi's. There was no grass and no dirt spaces on the ground, just clouds of green with purple, yellow, white, pink flowers, every kind of flower you could imagine. Vines climbed up every tall surface, like in Sleeping Beauty. The pond sparkled where it wasn't covered with lily pads, and every minute or so, a big green frog splashed in from the side, disappearing into the cool water.

And the chickens. How could anyone tell mean stories about them? These weren't the chickens you see in picture books. They were all different colours, some with fancy crowns and fluffy feather leg warmers.

"How do you keep this up by yourself?" Mama asked. Mimi said taking care of the garden and the chickens kept her young and gave her energy.

"This is my life's work," she said, matching Mama's eye twinkle. She brought us inside and let us help put the wildflowers into vases. We ate carrots and blueberries from her garden, and she made us tea from herbs she grew beside her house. Mama and Mimi chatted in that way that grown-up women do, and Freya added something every once in a while, but I sat frozen. The longer I was silent, the less I felt I could say anything.

Mama looked at her watch and said that we must get going. I had come all this way and not said a word to Mimi. It was now or never.

I opened my mouth and said something stupid. "Why does everyone think you're weird when your house is so cool?"

Awkward. I was burning with shame. But Mimi laughed. "Some people don't understand people who are different. There are lots of different ways to live in this world, and most of them are just as fine as any other. But folks don't know their options. They see what's in front of them, and they follow it. That's OK, if it works for them. But I knew that a certain kind of life wasn't going to work for me. We have to follow what's inside, girls. And sometimes just a few other special people will understand."

Once we made it out of hearing distance, we talked nonstop, even Mama.

"Can you believe how cute those chickens are?"

"Do you think she swims in the pond? Do you think she gets lonely?" Back on the path, everything looked the same, but felt completely different. The light, the air. Mimi showed me possibilities I didn't know existed.

The next day at school, Bernie was ready. "I heard you and your weird friend went to Mimi's! You should move there. I heard she's a witch. You'd probably get along."

Bernie's idea of the world is small. It's so small, it doesn't have room for Mimi. Or room for me. That's OK. Mimi's world is huge and full of magic, and I'd rather fit there anyway.

I've stopped responding to Bernie. He still says mean stuff, but his voice takes up much less space in my head. I have other things to think about anyway. I'm helping Mimi build a tree fort for me and Freya to use when we visit.

The Monster of Birch Lake

by Caroline Bennett

B reakfast!" called Dad. Sofia groaned. She didn't want to get out of bed. She curled up on her bunk and stared out of the cabin window. Sofia traced the window ledge with one hand, rested her head on the other, and sighed. The lake water was sparkling, tempting her to jump in. But that wasn't going to happen—not after what unfolded last summer. Sofia scowled at the dusty bucket of sand toys in her closet. She frowned at the brand-new swimming goggles and flippers hanging on the back of the bedroom door. She sighed again.

Sofia and her family had arrived at the cabin the night before. Every year, they rented the same one on Birch Lake. Sofia loved her friends there. The Splash Squad spent most of their time either in or on the lake. When they weren't in the water just splashing around, they went diving and kayaking. They raced on the beach and climbed on the rocks by the shore. But this year there was no way she was going in the lake, and she didn't think she could tell her friends why.

Sofia shuffled into the kitchen for breakfast.

"Burritos with eggs and cheese?" Dad asked. Sofia nodded and he poured her a glass of orange juice. They sat in silence at first. Her dad wouldn't talk to anyone until he'd had his second cup of coffee.

"Noah's gone to the beach to meet Malik, and Mum's gone to work," Dad said. When they drove in last night, her younger brother made plans with his friend in the cabin next door. Mum made the hour-long drive back and forth to Sudbury every day for work. Dad worked from home, so Sofia and Noah were able to hang out with friends at the lake all day.

The Splash Squad was older now and had more freedom. They didn't have to stay so close to the adults or to the other kids. The younger ones had to stay just outside the cabins on the beach. They built sandcastles, caught frogs, and paddled in the shallows while one of the adults kept an eye on them. The older kids paired up and kayaked to Bear Island. Sofia and her friends, right in the middle, went searching for snakes in the rocks, had water fights, or played Duck, Duck, Splash.

We are really lucky to be out of the city, Sofia thought. Matthew and Priyanka had to go to summer school. If I was at home, I'd be stuck watching Noah so Dad could work.

Sofia should have been super excited to be at the lake again, but not today. It was going to be a long summer.

The telephone rang. Sofia froze. She lifted the phone to her ear and winced.

"Hey! I saw you drive in last night. Are you swimming with us today? Lily and Eli are here too." It was her friend Ana. "Don't forget it's my birthday on Thursday. Did you get the party invitation?"

In the summer, Ana and Sofia called each other almost every day, but this year, Sofia had some excuses ready.

I have to go and visit my grandparents today.

I have a dentist appointment today.

I'm going with my brother to Science North today.

These things could be true, and everyone had days away from the camp… but Sofia would need to find even more reasons to avoid the lake.

"Hi, Ana," Sofia answered. "I'll be at the beach soon. I'm just getting ready. And of course, I remember! Your party's going to be awesome."

Sofia really loved to swim. Just not in Birch Lake. The lake was huge. She could barely see across to the other side. The lake was cold. The water wasn't heated like the pool at the community centre. The lake had animals living in it: crabs, jellyfish, even sharks! She knew this was ridiculous and untrue. She knew those creatures didn't live in lakes, but that didn't stop her worrying.

After what had happened last summer, Sofia panicked at the thought of going into the water. For the final week of their vacation last year, she stayed on the shore and told her friends that she wasn't feeling well. She tried everything to get over her fear. Her family tried to help too. Sofia's mum played tag with her at the water's edge, but Sofia only went in ankle deep. Her father challenged her to a race. In spite of her competitive streak, she turned him down. When her grandparents visited, her grandmother walked into the water with Sofia clinging to her like a spider monkey. She just couldn't let go.

It all started with the weeds at the bottom of the lake.

"Let's take a swim out to the dock, Sofia," Dad said. She and the other kids often paddled there in kayaks to swim and dive in the deeper water where the dock was anchored. It was the furthest she had ever swum before, but Dad was right beside her and that felt great. Sofia was determined. When she touched the slimy side of the wooden dock, she yipped and yelled, "I made it!"

Dad climbed up the ladder first, and Sofia scrambled up behind him. They sat on the edge of the dock. They dipped their feet in the cool water as they basked in the sun. Sofia closed her eyes and relaxed.

"How about you show me some of those dives you've been learning?" Dad suggested. Sofia loved to dive. She was the first in her swimming class to take the plunge from the highest platform.

"Cannonball!" Sofia yelled. After a few rounds of trying to make the biggest splash, they took turns diving to see who could get the farthest from the dock before coming up for air. Finally, they decided to see who could dive down the deepest. Dad went first. When he popped up, he threw a handful of weeds at Sofia. "Yuck!" she screamed, laughing. Now it was her turn.

Sofia took two running steps to the edge of the dock. With arms tight on either side of her head and her back straight, she leapt as high as she could, tucked up her knees, and hit the water with barely a splash. Her dive was perfect. She could see the bottom of the lake clearly through her goggles. She scooped through the water, kicking her legs as hard as she could. She reached the lake floor and grabbed a handful of weeds. When Sofia spun around to swim back to the surface, she saw something moving out of the corner of her eye. At first, she thought it was her dad, but quickly realized it wasn't.

The creature swimming towards her was murky green, huge and shaped like a torpedo. It had light spots over its dark body and was about a metre long. Sofia flailed her way up. When she reached the surface, she screamed. The dock was

19

only a few feet away and she swam for it wildly. As she touched the ladder, she felt something sharp tug on her leg. Her dad hauled her up, and Sofia started crying.

"It bit me! Look." They both watched the creature flash by the dock, its fins and tail swishing.

"That is a big fish, Sofia. But I don't think it bit you. Let me see."

Blood dripped down Sofia's leg. Dad used his goggles to scoop up some water and wash it off. "You've got a bit of a cut there. I don't think it's too bad. But let's get back to the cabin and clean it up. Do you think you can make it?"

"I don't know," whimpered Sofia. Getting back in the water terrified her. But how else would she get to shore?

"How about you put your arms around my shoulders. I'll swim with you on my back."

"Okay," Sofia said, wiping away her tears. She stood up and took some slow deep breaths. Dad jumped in the water and made lots of splashing movements to scare away the fish. "I think it's gone, but we'll go fast," he said.

Sofia slid into the water, wrapping her arms around her father like a baby possum. It took forever, but Sofia could finally see the sandy bottom of the shallows. She let go of her dad and splashed the last few feet to safety through the gentle waves breaking on the beach.

So, this summer, what was she going to do? All her friends would expect her to rush into the lake the first chance she had. Sofia had to find ways to avoid the water.

On the first day, she held up some garbage bags and suggested to the Splash Squad that they clean up the beach before they went swimming. All kinds of things washed up on shore. Plastic drink bottles, cans, and other trash came from boaters who tossed things overboard. Her friends loved that idea. They collected two black bags full of rubbish, and three blue bags of recyclables. They threw the bags in the dumpsters at the back of the Camp General Store.

"Great job!" said Mrs. Davis, who owned the store. She gave each of them a pop as a reward. Sofia was part of her school's Eco Club, so it felt great to help the environment. After the cleanup, Sofia, Ana, and their dads went to the grocery store in Espanola to get supplies. Success! Day One was over, and no swimming!

The next day it rained—luckily. "Board Game Day!" yelled Sofia. The families brought out games like chess, Scrabble, and Catan. They also had cards to play games like Euchre. Ana's mum was a card shark. No one could beat her at Euchre, and she told the kids that she would never let them win unless they earned it. While they had fun, they told funny stories about things that happened to them over the past year, and Sofia decided to share.

"Hey, let me tell you about something that happened here last summer." Her friends stared at her. She took a deep breath and told them all about the lake monster. "Dad thinks that I cut myself on the ladder of the dock, but I know that monster bit me."

"That's crazy," Lily said.

"Nightmare!" yelled Eli. "I can't wait to go looking for it!"

"I don't think that's a good idea," Sofia said. "It's really big."

"It's not bigger than us, and now we know, we can keep our eyes open for it," Eli replied.

He has a point, thought Sofia, But I'm still staying out of the lake. She smiled at her friends and nodded, as if agreeing with their plans. Inside, she shook with fear. Still, Day Two was over, and no swimming!

On the third day, Sofia went with her mother into Sudbury to check out some new books from the library. She was part of their summer reading club. While they were in Sudbury, Sofia had lunch with her grandparents and stayed at their house until Mum finished work. When they got back to the camp, Sofia had just enough time to go to the camp store to pick up a treat. It was too late for swimming, so Day Three had ended. Success!

It took barely a minute to get from Sofia's family cabin to the store. Mrs. Davis sold penny candy at the counter for the children. The candy didn't really cost a penny, but all the children in the camp called it that. The camp had been there for years and so had the corner store. Sofia was choosing from the jars of sour keys and candy bracelets when Mr. Davis came in. He welcomed her back to Birch Lake with a hug and then said, "I hear you had a run in with Sir Patrick last summer."

"Who's Sir Patrick?" Sofia asked.

"The big old Northern Pike that hangs out in the weeds in the deeper water. He's always looking for something to eat, but he never goes for people. He prefers to eat walleyes, but he's not too fussy! Sir Patrick is at the top of the food chain here and he'll eat just about anything. Even frogs, snakes, birds, and bugs!"

"Why do you think it was Sir Patrick?" Sofia wanted to know.

"Well, from what your dad told me, it was him for sure. But I agree with your dad, I doubt he bit you." Mr. Davis pointed at a poster on the wall. It was all about the Northern Pike. "Did it look like that?" he asked. Sofia nodded. "That's it!" Mr. Davis took the poster down, rolled it up and handed it to Sofia. "You can have this," he said.

Sofia chose a candy bracelet, put it on her wrist, and waved at the Davises as she left the store. When she got back to the cabin she taped the poster up in her room, on the wall by the closet. She stared at it for what felt like forever.

The next day was Thursday, Ana's birthday. Her family's plan was a barbecue on the beach. There would be food, cake, presents, games and, of course, swimming. Sofia still didn't know how to avoid going in the water. Even though she had told her friends what had happened, and how scared she had been, she knew that they would expect her to jump right in. Sofia couldn't sleep. All night long she thought about the problem. How am I going to have fun at the party if I don't go swimming? How can I go in the lake and not be terrified?

Just after the sun rose, Sofia's eyes landed on the poster on the wall again. "I've got it," she said out loud. She collected everything she needed. When her dad called her for breakfast, she was ready! She carefully waddled out of her room.

"Wow!" her dad exclaimed. "That is some outfit!"

"What on earth…?" said her mum.

Sofia had on a long-sleeved black t-shirt, black leggings, and her black biking gloves. On her feet were flippers, and a snorkel and mask covered most of her smiling face, leaving only her chin visible. "I'm an underwater explorer," she explained. She held up her inflatable water mattress, which she had blown up by herself.

After breakfast, the whole family walked down to the beach where the Splash Squad and their families were gathered. Sofia's friends took one look at her, and decided to get their floaties, snorkels and masks too. They spent a couple of hours floating around with just their heads underwater. They even paddled out to the dock. Sofia volunteered to be the judge of her friend's dives. That way she could keep a watch out for Sir Patrick. As she sat in safety on the dock, she made a list in her head about what she knew.

★ Northern Pikes might have sharp teeth, but they don't eat people. If she had been delicious, Sir Patrick would have held on tight to get a good chunk.

★ Northern Pikes lurk in the weeds on the lake bed waiting for prey to come to them. Sir Patrick only came out of the weeds because she and Dad had disturbed his spot.

★ Her explorer's outfit would protect her from Sir Patrick. The black colour would not attract his attention, and he would get a mouthful of leggings if he tried to bite.

★ The Splash Squad would be noisy and discourage any creature from coming close. Her mum always said Sofia and her friends had to stay 10 feet away from her when she was watching them play, so Sir Patrick would probably feel the same way!

That's it! Sofia decided, I am not going to let Sir Patrick take away my love of this beautiful place.

"Cannonball!" she yelled, jumping into the water. She stayed close to the dock and kept a sharp eye out, but her outfit seemed to work. When it was time to head back, Sofia took a deep breath and looked at the shore, way in the distance.

"Do you want to use my pool mattress?" Sofia asked Lily. Lily only had half a pool noodle. Her dog had eaten the rest.

"Really? Are you sure?" Lily asked.

"Absolutely! I want to swim back without it." Before she could change her mind, Sofia did a scuba diver's backwards jump into the water. It felt great! Her flippers helped her swim fast, and her snorkel and mask let her keep an eye open for Sir Patrick. She was first back to shore.

The Splash Squad ate burgers, hotdogs, chips and dip, watermelon, and chocolate birthday cake. After lunch, they played a game of volleyball and then got back in the water. Sofia left her flippers on shore.

Over the next few weeks, Sofia redesigned her explorer's outfit. She wore goggles instead of her snorkel and mask. She put on a black T-shirt with her leggings. Then, her swimsuit with her leggings. Then it was black shorts with her swimsuit. By the last week of the summer, Sofia was back to swimming in just her swimsuit.

When she next went to the library, Sofia signed out books about animals that live in lakes. The more she read, the less she worried. The lake was full of aquatic creatures, and each had their part to play in the ecosystem. And even though Sir Patrick was still roaming around Birch Lake and might be living there for several more years, Sofia was comfortable sharing the beauty and joy of the water with him. She just hoped that monster would never bite her again!

The Other Side of the Island

by Latoya Belfon

Summer was here, and school was finally out. Cora's first year as a high school student was incredible and scary, and she was happy it was over. Her English teacher, Ms. Brenda, asked her to use the summer to discover something new and write about it.

"She just couldn't leave us without an assignment, huh? Sigh!" she thought as she packed her notepad in her bag and left the bustling school grounds.

Ms. Brenda called out cheerfully to the class as they left.

"This should be fun! Happy summer, little writers!"

Cora smirked. Knowing how much of a perfectionist she was, she wasn't sure how much fun she'd actually have writing the assignment. Either way, determined to get a head start on her report, she ventured to her favourite summer spot— Marquis Beach.

Cora lived on Solonã Island, a small island in the Caribbean known for its beautiful beaches and cheery people. With little else to do, going to the beach was one of the most exciting summer activities. You never know what might wash up in the waves onto the white sand of Marquis Beach.

The beach was packed with many families on the first day of summer vacation. Balls flew through the air, and dogs chased each other, defending their territory. Although the blue, crystal-clear waves were calling out to Cora, there was barely a spot where she could dive in and feel the cool water over her head on this hot summer day. She sat on the beach, using her mother's yellow and white-striped market umbrella to shade herself from the piercing sun. She fanned away the heat with her community's newsletter, stopping only to quickly read that Seashore Grillz Resto was offering a summer promo on "Fry Fish and Bakes."

"Ugh! How can I complete my summer assignment when I can't even get close to the water?" she said as her frustration grew.

Cora thought that if she used the first week of summer to write a stellar report, she could relax and do whatever she wanted for the rest of the season. She believed that something spectacular was bound to wash up on the shore, and she could write a fabulous discovery story about it. But, with the beach so crowded, she could barely see the shoreline.

She imagined Ms. Brenda's response. "What happened, Miss Vincent? B+? Very disappointing!" She imagined the class laughing hysterically at her failure and pointing their judgy fingers at her. With a quick shake of her shoulders, snapping her back to reality, she admitted to the low probability of things happening like that and knew Ms. Brenda wouldn't say such a thing. However, she wouldn't be happy with a B+, so she needed to think quickly. Suddenly, out of the corner of her eye, she saw a group of older teenagers huddled together, whispering. Do they have a secret? Are they concocting a devious plan? They looked around suspiciously to make sure no one was watching. Then, they quietly walked toward the right side of the beach, disappearing behind a thick cluster of coconut trees, and climbed up a steep, dusty hill that jutted out into the sea. They had bags on their backs, as if they were going camping. Cora had never ventured that far down the beach and often wondered where people were going when she saw them climb that steep hill. Come to think of it, she had never really seen anyone come back from that hill, either. "Maybe this is the adventure I need to have for my summer report? What do I do? I can't go alone. My brother must know where these teenagers are off to," she whispered.She hurried off to find her brother in the sea of beachgoers, determined to find proof that she had just stumbled upon the best summer report idea Ms. Brenda would ever read. "Hey, Bro, I just saw a group of kids your age going down by the far side of the beach and up the hill. Where are they going?" she asked, eagerly anticipating his response. He stared at her with a mysterious look in his eyes. What did he know? And why wasn't he telling her?

"Tell me, William! Please!"

The wait was unbearable. She started to envision what might be beyond that hill. Could it lead to a hidden treasure trove? Could it be a secret part of the island that had fewer rowdy beachgoers and a better chance of getting into the water?

Her brother stopped her and revealed the mysteries that awaited beyond the hill.

"It is just the other side of the island," he said casually.

"The other side of the island? So why don't many people go there?" she asked.

"It's a steep climb and steep drag down. Most people don't want to take the chance of tumbling down the hill and being pierced by sharp, massive rocks."

"Have you ever gone there? Can we go? I have to see it myself!"

William's friends came over to hear what they were discussing. Excited about the chance to venture up that hill again, they convinced him to take the trip and bring her along the next day.

Her brother warned her that it would be a tough climb and that they couldn't tell their parents. With the sound of her mother's safety warnings ringing in her ears, she was unsure if this was the best decision.

Cora agreed to keep quiet but decided to leave a note in her mom's book, knowing she'd find it during her daily 7:00 p.m. reading. Then, she would have kept her word to her brother and obeyed her mother.

The morning came, and Cora hurriedly packed her beach bag. Her mom was already up, spreading their colourfully patterned bed sheets over shrubs in the front yard, hoping to catch as much sunshine as possible. Their mother waved them off with kisses and a quick reminder to be safe, unaware of their plan to discover the other side of the island.

As they ran down the sandy tracks to Marquis Beach, Cora felt as though she was venturing to a completely new beach, a new island.

The beach was nearly empty, with only a few people and large rocks on beach towels, holding spaces for dedicated beachgoers. She didn't turn left as she usually would. As they walked to the right of the beach, the white sand gradually became brown and rocky, and soon they were at the bottom of the steep hill. Her brother's best friend huddled them together to give the final instructions. Cora looked around at her brother William, his best friend George and George's twin cousins, Kiki and Kirk.George told them to make sure their shoes were tied tightly and to grab onto the wild shrubs on the hill to help them climb. He also reminded them to stay low so that strong winds wouldn't blow them off the hill.He scanned their faces, looking for any sign of hesitation. They shook their heads in agreement. It was a steep, rugged climb—one that felt never-ending, as though the top would never be reached. Her back ached from holding a low posture. Soon, she heard George's victory chants—he had reached the top first. "Oh, sweet relief will soon be here," she thought. They reached the top and looked out at the clear blue skies, with clouds almost within arm's reach, and down at the vast ocean, where blue waves crashed onto the sharp-edged rocks. George hurried them off, as standing on the top was too risky. They made their way down the other side. Cora beamed at the beauty of this side of Solonã Island. The sand was whiter. It glistened in the sun as bright as the pearl rocks that dotted the shore. Cora and Kiki picked up the beautiful emerald-green glass stones, laughing and chatting about what they could do with them. Behind them, Kirk and William began a rowdy water fight, relishing the space and freedom of a private beach. In the midst of this merriment, George called out for everyone. He pointed toward something none of them had noticed before. "Another island?" Kiki asked, her voice full of excitement. "How do we get there?"

George pointed to a narrow path slowly revealing itself as the tide receded. "We can walk across while the tide is low," he explained.

Cora hesitated, unease creeping into her excitement. "Are you sure it's safe? We don't know how long the tide will stay low. What if we get stuck over there?"

William nodded in agreement. "Maybe we shouldn't risk it."

But before they could discuss further, Kiki and Kirk dashed ahead, laughing as they ran toward the mysterious new island. Their excitement was infectious, and soon George followed, urging the others to come along. Despite her doubts, Cora joined them, curiosity outweighing her fear.

They stood in awe, the new island unfolding like a dream before them. The sand was a soft pink, shimmering like tiny crystals under the sunlight. Strange, enormous mango trees dotted the landscape, their fruits as big as bowling balls. Lush vegetation surrounded them—humongous flowers, thick vines, and watermelons that were red on the outside. Pumpkins, usually orange, were an unusual shade of green.

The group wandered further into the island, marveling at the vibrant and surreal environment. The salty breeze carried the scent of ripe sea grapes. Cora plucked a few and savored their rare, tangy flavor. It had been a while since Cora had tasted sea grapes. They were usually green, but these were a rare pink, swaying gently in the wind.

"This place is unbelievable," she said, grinning as she picked more sea grapes. Kiki had already filled her hands with them, gulping down water to wash away the saltiness.

"Slow down," Cora warned her. "You might need that water later."

Kirk laughed. "What's the big deal? Home's just a hill climb away." He didn't seem to remember they'd crossed an ocean path to get here.

The group ventured deeper into the island, chattering excitedly about what to name their discovery. But as the hours passed, they realized they had drunk all their water, and the heat began to weigh on them.

"Anyone have any water left?" Cora asked, shaking her empty bottle. The others searched their bags, but it was the same for everyone. Just as they began to worry, the sky darkened without warning. Heavy storm clouds rolled in, blotting out the sun and casting an eerie shadow over the island.

Yet, somehow, stars appeared in the sky as well. Realizing that the storm would bring high tides, possibly blocking their path off the island, George grabbed his bag and jetted off.

"Let's go now! The tide is rising!" George screamed.

"I can't find my bag! Wait for me!" said Kiki.

"Forget your bag Kiki. The last thing we care about is a bag. Let's go!" said her brother Kirk.

They ran through tall, sharp razor grass. It scratched their legs and arms. The ground turned soft and mushy beneath them, causing slips and tumbles at every turn. Eventually, they reached the shoreline but couldn't see more than ten feet in front of them. There was no sign of Solonã Island or the crossing, as though both had vanished into thin air. The clouds burst with rain, and they ran off to find shelter under a cluster of banana trees. It was dark as night. It seemed they had waited for hours for the rain to cease. Cora thought her mother would read her note soon and look for them. This helped her remain calm. The rain eventually stopped, but it was still dark. They tried to return to the pink sand beach, but the path they had taken to the shoreline was nowhere to be found.

"I never wanted to do this," said Kiki crying.

"If I remember correctly, you and your brother ran over here before we decided if we should go as a group. It's your fault!" said George angrily.

"Well, you're the one who spotted this mysterious island! If you didn't, then we would already be back home!" said Kiki.

"Guys, this is not helping! We need to figure out what to do and where to go! There is no way for us to go back to where we came from. Do you think anyone's living on this strange island, George?" asked Cora.

"I don't see how anyone could live here. We have been wandering back and forth, and have not seen fresh water, no animals, not even a mosquito, so I don't know," he said.

"Well, we need to try to find out because people come here. Earlier today, I noticed some rose bushes looked cut, as if a gardener had been there. We should go back to that spot and see if there are any tracks," said Cora.

"I don't like this idea!" said Kiki.

They headed where they believed they had seen the rose bushes. Suddenly, the sun burst through the clouds.

"Is it afternoon? Wasn't it just nighttime?" Cora thought to herself.

Then the heat became unbearable. Tired, confused, and thirsty, they unknowingly wandered back to the beach, collapsed under a small palm tree, and dozed off.

They were awoken by the bustle of people walking through the bushes. It was morning, but it didn't feel like they slept through the night. Cora wondered if they were trapped in a time warp. Nothing made sense.

Then, in the distance, they saw hotel workers setting up beach umbrellas. The workers spotted them and ushered them over.

"The kids' activities are starting soon, so maybe you all should head back. The beach is booked for these guests for the morning," she said in her Americanized receptionist voice.

"Wait, did she say morning? We have got to get home!" Cora said, panicking.

George didn't want the workers to suspect they didn't belong, so he responded in his version of an American accent.

"Actually, one of you was supposed to bring us beverages to the beach, like my parents ordered. But I'll let it go. Just take us back to the hotel immediately!"

The hotel worker nodded, fearing retaliation. The group glared at each other, unable to believe that George's devout imitation of famous American actors' accents had paid off. The workers took them along a trail of palm trees on the edge of a well-maintained concrete road, lined with garden lights and manicured plants. They had explored many parts of this mysterious island but had never seen this place.

"Where did this come from?" Cora whispered.

The hotel workers directed them to the reception area, where the receptionist greeted them by their full names and gave them drinks. How did they know their names? A chill crept down Cora's spine. They put their drinks down nervously, scanned for a quick exit, then dashed through the resort, looking for a way out. The receptionist chased them, forbidding them from leaving, and insisting that they drink the beverage. They ran until they found a door that opened onto what seemed like a village street. Then soon some sites became familiar. They ran past Marquis Beach and knew they were close to their homes. Relieved, they hugged each other and said goodbye, unaware of the punishment that awaited them.

Cora and William expected to see the police and a search unit gathered outside of their parents' home. Instead, their mother was outside, chatting with a neighbor and folding dry laundry.

"You're back so soon?" asked their mother, eyeing them with stern curiosity.

"Mom, it didn't rain? What time is it?" asked Cora.

"No, it has been burning hot all day. It's almost 2:00 p.m." said her mom cheerfully.

"But the hotel workers on the island said good morning," Cora thought with a puzzled look. Nothing made sense to Cora and William. It felt as though they had been gone for two days. They ran to their mother and hugged her tightly, relieved to be home safely.

Cora went to her room and closed the door. She had a lot to write about, but a trail of questions plagued her mind.

"Did the hotel workers try to force us to drink the beverage so we would forget the island? Is this why no one has ever spoken about it? You forget once you leave? Why were the fruits so different? An island with no animals or insects? Why did the hotel workers assume we were guests at the hotel? Why were there stars in the sky during a storm? Why couldn't we see Solonã Island even after the storm had gone? We crossed the ocean to this mysterious island, but somehow, a door in a hotel led us back to Solonã. How did we return so quickly without a boat or without crossing the ocean again?"

As she wrote, a new thought struck her—she remembered the note she had left in her mother's book. Sneaking into the living room, she carefully opened the book and saw the note still there, untouched. Relief washed over her as she realized her mom would never know what they had done.

Her heart skipped a beat as she heard her mother call out from the kitchen. "I feel like eating some pink sea grapes," she said casually.

Cora froze. How could her mother know about the pink sea grapes?

She clutched her notebook tightly, questions swirling in her mind. Whatever mysteries the other side of the island held, she knew one thing for sure— this was only the beginning of a much bigger mystery.

Murphy

by Deborah Ross-Attas

My parents completely ruined my morning when they broke the news that we were moving again.

"But you promised this move would be the last," I said.

"We know. We feel awful about breaking that promise, but this opportunity is too good for your dad to turn down. In fact, it will change a lot of things for all of us. It means we can buy a house," said Mom.

"I don't care!"

"We can take a real family vacation," she said.

"I don't care!"

"We can even take you and Essie to Disney World," added Dad. "Like you've been talking about."

I was about to say I don't care again when I thought it might be cool to see the Star Wars-themed park. But instead of giving in to the bright side, I shouted at my parents.

"I've finally got friends here and the Taekwondo tournament is in three weeks. You know I've been training forever. I don't care about a house or a trip. I hate you both! You can't make me go."

Tears filled my eyes, and my cheeks burned. My parents' faces changed as my words spilled out.

"You need to go to your room," said Dad.

"You don't care about me!" I shot back.

"Go to your room," he repeated slowly in his serious voice.

I stomped down the hall and slammed the bedroom door before throwing myself face down on Essie's bottom bunk. My head hurt from crying and I couldn't catch my breath. Moving meant I wouldn't finish grade four with my besties—Edmund, Olivia, and Farnaz. Maybe I'd suffocate in the wet pillow that was getting wetter with every tear. Strange, my ears were getting wet too. Then I felt a tongue licking my ear. Lifting my head, I looked into two big eyes staring back at me.

"Hey boy, where did you come from? I asked, sliding off the mattress onto the floor.

I ruffled the fur on his ears and neck, wondering how he got into the building with a "NO DOGS ALLOWED" sign posted at the front entrance.

Our apartment was on the first floor, so he might have walked in behind another tenant and wandered along the hall to our door.

"Hey buddy do you have a name? Where's your owner? How'd you get in here?"

And that's when it happened.

"Murphy's the name."

"Wait, did you just say something? No, this isn't possible. Dogs don't talk!"

"Actually we do. People just don't listen," came a slow and gravelly reply.

"You do? How's it possible? Where did you come from?" I had a gazillion more questions to ask but Essie pushed open the bedroom door and walked over to sit beside me on the floor. I panicked. Mom and Dad would freak out if Essie ran and told them about the dog.

"Onyu, don't be sad," she said.

"Essie, don't tell mom and dad about the dog. OK?"

"OK, no dog," she answered, looking at me strangely.

Murphy must have left the room and the apartment, which was a good thing.

The move took place five days later. Thankfully, I got to say goodbye to Edmund, Olivia and Farnaz. We promised to keep in touch. I didn't see Murphy again in the neighbourhood or around the apartment. That was a sure sign I must have been dreaming. And Essie never said anything about seeing a dog.

"Onyu, is your backpack ready?" Mom called from our new kitchen.

"Yup."

"Your lunch?"

"Got it."

"Runners for gym?"

"Uh-huh."

"Water bottle?"

"Ditto."

Entering grade four at the end of April would be tough. Everyone had been together for months already and friendships were already tight. Once again, I'd be the new kid and probably the shortest in the class. That's why I took Taekwondo in every city we'd moved to. Dad would say, "You're likely going to be the shortest, so you have to learn to defend yourself."

I'm pretty good and hoped a club was near our new home. On top of that, I knew I was going to get teased about my name Onyu. I got called OnWho, OnWu, and my least

favourite, Oh Youhoo! gets to me!

After Mom registered Essie and me, two students came down from Mr. Bilmes's grade four-five to lead me to class.

"Hey, I'm Delsa."

"I'm Zehra, what's your name?" asked the girl with the black glasses.

"ON YU!" I shouted, which may have sounded rude but I was trying to make it clear what my name was.

We arrived at Room 206 on the second floor. My heart raced as I entered, not knowing who or what I was going to face. Mr. Bilmes looked friendly as he pointed to a desk and chair midway across the room, in a group with three other students.

The clock above the class door showed it was already 10:45. Recess, math, then lunch according to the schedule on the whiteboard.

"Hey, new kid, want to sit with us at lunch?" whispered the boy beside me.

"Sure," I smiled back.

I felt relieved I wouldn't be alone during lunch. Maybe things would go smoothly. Like Dad said, "You've got to be positive. You smile and they'll smile back."

But it didn't work that way. The cafeteria was a large gym with a stage at one end for assemblies. Each grade had a long table with the teacher's name taped to it. Mr. Bilmes's table was packed and there was no room to squeeze in. All the kids from the classes who didn't fit, had to sit on the steps that led to the stage. I joined them.

"Hey, leftover, what ya eating? Leftovers?" called out one of the boys from my class.

When I looked over at the table, my classmates were laughing. I realized that's what all the kids on the stage steps were called, The Leftovers!

I kept my head down and focused on eating my spaghetti. I didn't look left or right. I kept my eyes on the red sauce, certain my face matched it.

If the rest of the year was going to be like lunch, I was doomed. There were two parts to lunch, the eating part and the playing part. I walked around the schoolyard trying to look friendly. I asked to join the boys playing soccer.

"We've already got our teams," one replied.

I went to the playground area with the slides and swings. I hoped to find someone to play tag with, only to find out it was day three and only grade three students were allowed in. I don't usually mind being alone, but walking around by myself advertised I had no friends. I was a leftover! I noticed a treed area at the far end of the yard. Maybe I could get lost over there until the bell rang. I sat on the ground with my back against a tree and closed my eyes. A little nap couldn't hurt.

41

Slurp.

"Ewwwww! What the heck?" I wiped my face; certain I'd been slimed only to find a wet nose and a pair of brown eyes staring at me.

"Murphy? Is it really you? How'd you find me? Wow! I'm glad to see you! You may be the only friend I'll ever have at this place. Say something boy," I hugged him and buried my face in his neck.

"Ruff, ruff," was all that came out.

"Hey, Onyu."

Lifting my head, I saw Delsa and Zehra waving at me to join them.

Were they afraid of dogs and didn't want to come closer? And why didn't Murphy talk? Was I dreaming back at the apartment?

I jumped up, brushing dog hair off my pants as I walked over to them. "See you later boy."

"We need someone to turn the ropes so we can practice our tricks for the talent show," said Delsa.

"What talent show?" I asked.

"You'll find out more this afternoon at rehearsal. We have to participate for the fundraiser."

"Everybody's already signed up except Toby."

OMG, my stomach did a flip and I felt weak at the knees. Surely being the new kid I wasn't expected to participate, especially since they were already rehearsing.

"Hey, Dylan! Come help turn for us," shouted Zehra.

I turned my head and saw a tall skinny kid with a mop of black hair coming towards us.

"Sure," he said smiling. "Onyu, grab the other end of the rope and we can work our magic."

I did what he said. I was so terrified that I would have to be in the talent show, I was having an out-of-body experience. My turning arm wasn't cooperating and the girls stumbled.

"Sorry. My fault."

"Hey, leftover, guess you ate noodles cause your noodle arm is useless."

"Toby, mind your business. Try it again Onyu," encouraged Dylan.

Thankfully, the bell rang and rescued me from further embarrassment. As we lined up to go back inside, I turned my head to check if Murphy was still by the trees. He was. I nodded and I swear he did too. I think he smiled. I felt a little better knowing he was there.

That afternoon I learned more about the talent show. Each class was fundraising to help pay for buses to take the whole school on a fun-filled day trip to a nature site. Some classes were selling cookies for a dollar and some were selling freezies. Mr. Bilmes's class was charging a dollar for talent show tickets. And I found out that I had to go on stage and perform. But what could I do? I didn't sing, dance, or play an instrument. I sat at the back of the gymnasium hoping I was invisible.

"Onyu, could you come here?" asked Mr. Bilmes. He wasn't really asking me.

"Yes sir," I replied, heading to the stage.

"Onyu, I know you don't have much time before the show to prepare, so is there a talent you'd be comfortable sharing?"

"Not really," I answered.

"That figures," called out Toby.

"That's enough Toby," said Mr. Bilmes in a stern voice.

"Can you do magic tricks?" Mr. Bilmes asked trying to help me out.

I shrugged. "I take Taekwondo?"

"So does Toby," Mr. Bilmes said. "That could work! Toby, that's good news. You and Onyu can put together a demo of TKD moves." Mr. Bilmes walked over to where Toby sat looking very unhappy and said, "You need to cooperate."

I had four days to practice with Toby, who clearly didn't like me. The rest of the class was used to ignoring him. He was way bigger than me—in height and weight. If he fell on me, I'd be like Flat Stanley. We were given time in the afternoon to work together on our moves but Toby horsed around and I was too scared to tell on him. I did my best to suggest some kicks and blocks, but Toby just laughed.

"You worry too much. Just follow me and do what I do. I'll be the master and you the student."

"We've got to practice or the audience will laugh at us. We're supposed to be the finale," I pleaded.

"Look, I know what I'm doing. Just wear your uniform and we'll give them a show like they've never seen before. You're gonna be surprised how good I am."

"Is Toby going to use me as his personal target? I can't take it! Murphy, what do I do?" I asked under my breath.

The night before the show I was finishing up my science homework. I smelled Murphy before I saw him.

"Murphy, you keep popping in and out. Maybe you should be in the talent show. The Magical Dog!"

"I need help Murphy. The kid I'm supposed to practice with keeps telling me not to worry but that makes me worry even more. It's bad enough being at the leftover table; I don't need to be made fun of too in front of everyone!"

"What are you thinking?" asked Murphy.

"I can demo all kinds of moves. I've already picked out the music, but Toby just says, "Yeah, yeah, blah, blah.""

"You know what I would do?" Murphy asked with a toothy grin.

"Talk to my teacher?"

"That's not what I was going to say, but let's go with it. A much safer idea."

Early the next morning, I made a jelly sandwich to eat on the way to school and grabbed my backpack with my TKD uniform and blue belt. Murphy was right, I had to speak to Mr. Bilmes and hope that maybe, just maybe, Mr. Bilmes would say I didn't have to be in it.

Only a few kids were playing in the schoolyard, their parents watching them. I didn't see anyone I knew, so I started to enter the double doors.

"Hey, Onyu, why the sad face?" asked Delsa. "Gotta have positive energy for the show this afternoon."

"Yeah, about that, I'm not feeling too good," I replied holding my stomach and hoping I looked sick enough to be sent home and wouldn't have to perform with Toby.

"It's just nerves. Everybody feels like that. Even me," she said.

"But Toby's not your partner. I've gotta go and find Mr. Bilmes."

"Want company?"

"Thanks, but I want to speak to him on my own." I headed up to the second floor.

Mr. Bilmes was sitting at his desk.

"Onyu, you're early!" He smiled.

"I don't think I can do the talent show," I said.

"What's the problem?"

"Well, Toby won't practice and we haven't got a routine planned. He keeps saying he knows what he's doing. But I don't know what he's doing." I hung my head and waited, hoping Mr. Bilmes would say the magic words I wanted to hear.

"Onyu, just do your best. Get up on that stage and do what you feel comfortable doing. Remember, it's a fundraiser. Have fun. Play the music you chose and put on a show. You and Toby don't have to do the same thing."

Mr. Bilmes and Delsa must have been from another planet. Be positive? Have fun? Enjoy? How could I enjoy when I was terrified of getting hurt and looking like a fool.

Three o'clock was show-time and I had to escape. Too bad I wasn't like Murphy and could disappear.

I watched the clock all morning. Time was passing too slowly and whenever I looked over at Toby, he raised his eyebrows and grinned. What was that supposed to mean?

I couldn't eat lunch. I sat on the stage steps with the others staring into space.

"Earth to Onyu," said Dylan. "What's up with you?"

"I'm a little nervous."

"Has it got anything to do with Toby?"

"Yeah, Mr. Bilmes thinks I need to, 'enjoy the moment'," I said.

"Try ignoring Toby. Do what you do best. If you're a blue belt, you've got moves," said Dylan.

He's right. I've got moves. I'd even won medals for my patterns at tournaments. I could run rings around Toby.

"Dylan, you're a genius," I said, as I made my way over to Mrs. Thompson, the lunch lady, to ask permission to stay behind after she dismissed the kids.

Instead of going out to play, I mapped out the stage like a math grid—Mr. Bilmes would've been proud. I decided which move to perform in each square. I needed space for kicks and spins. I didn't want to fall off the stage or on my face. I kept on practicing, hearing the music in my head. Then the afternoon bell rang. Two hours until the talent show. Two hours to run through my routine silently in my mind.

"OK class, gather up all your materials and props for the show," shouted Mr. Bilmes. "You can't come back to the class if you've forgotten anything, so don't forget."

"Oh my gosh, I'm so nervous. What if I goof up the skipping steps?" asked Zehra.

"You won't. I know you won't. It will all be good," piped Delsa.

I hoped so. From Delsa's lips to the ears of the talent show gods.

We all had to wait in the outer hallway, then enter the stage at the lunchroom door, up the steps to take our positions. I listened to the applause and waited as each group of students did their act. My heart raced. I'd changed into my white uniform and tied my blue belt in the traditional knot.

Toby hung back and wasn't dressed in his uniform. What was he waiting for? There were only a few more acts to go. The emcee announced Delsa and Zehra's skipping number. I gave them a silent high-five and mouthed, "You go!"

Two more acts until we were up. I walked over to Toby who was sitting on the floor and noticed he was breathing kinda funny.

"Aren't you going to change?" I asked.

"No… I forgot my uniform," he replied struggling to catch his breath.

"That's ok. You don't really need one."

Toby slumped over. His breathing was ragged. His eyes were glazed. He sounded like Essie when she had an asthma attack.

"Mr. Bilmes," I called. "Quick. Toby's in trouble. He can't breathe."

That's when I heard the emcee introduce Toby and me. I didn't want to leave Toby but the Kung Fu Panda intro was playing.

Feeling frantic, I heard Murphy say, "The show must go on."

"Boy, am I glad to see you."

"Get out there, Onyu. You can do this. Just do it like you did at lunch. You were awesome."

"You saw me?"

"No time to explain. Just get out there."

"Who you talking to?" the emcee asked and signaled me to go.

"I can do this. I can do this," I repeated to myself. I headed to the stage but watched over my shoulder as Mr. Bilmes called 911 and paged the principal. I focused and found my position. I took a deep breath, then…BAM! I moved to the music like a master.

I started with a flying side kick, then a spinning hook kick, a few ax kicks and back kicks. Boy was I flying. The kids whistled and clapped to the beat of the music. At the end, I leapt off the stage, landing with one knee up and one knee down in a bow.

The crowd went crazy. I stood and bowed again.

I joined my classmates who were huddled together in the outer hall looking worried, watching Toby being taken away on a stretcher by paramedics. The audience hadn't seen or heard anything because the music was loud and my moves distracted them. So it wasn't until the next day that the school found out about Toby.

Mr. Bilmes explained, "Toby had an anxiety attack."

Whoa, I thought I was anxious. It turns out that I did a good thing by keeping all eyes on me. Who would have thought?

Walking through the halls that day, all kinds of kids and teachers called out, "Great job!"

Essie's class all ran and hugged me. Embarrassing!

Two days later, Toby returned to school. I was ready for his teasing at lunch calling me a leftover. I wondered how Murphy would handle him.

Dylan, Delsa and I were sitting on the stage steps, going over the talent show plans for next year. Toby headed towards us.

Murphy whispered in my ear, "Don't react. Smile."

I took a deep yoga breath and let it out.

"Hey, Onyu, I hear you saved the day. Can I sit up there with you guys?" asked Toby.

I almost fell over. By the looks on Delsa and Dylan's faces, I'm sure they were thinking the same. Who is this person? Did an alien switch him?

I managed to mumble, "You know you'll be called a leftover? Right?"

"Yeah. That's OK, I like leftovers when you really think about it. Pizza for breakfast? It's the best."

"I like pizza for breakfast too. But what's really the best, are warmed up pancakes with syrup."

Murphy licked his lips in agreement, as Toby unknowingly sat right beside him.

Ravenous

by Julianne Mundle

Jerome

I smiled with pride as I stood in the living room. The recording confirmed that I had detention that day at 2:30 p.m. for thirty minutes. I had intercepted the call. My parents would never know. About an hour later, the garage door opened, signalling that my parents were home.

They entered the house through our large side door.

"How was school today?" Dad asked as he placed his backpack on the floor. I gave him a hug.

"It was great, Daddy." He wore a stained black polo shirt and blue denim pants, and he smelled of motor oil. He owned a mechanic shop called James Mechanic Station.

"Why do you have stains on your clothes?" I asked.

"I helped the boys with some cars today."

Mom walked up behind Dad, dropped her briefcase, removed her beige heels, and gave me a quick peck on my cheek.

"So, school was great you said, sweetie?"

I nodded.

"I got a call from the school today that said otherwise," she replied flatly.

I wanted the earth to swallow me up. My parents gave me disapproving stares. I was busted.

"I can explain."

"Go ahead," Dad said, his arms folded.

"It wasn't my fault. This kid at school bullies me daily so I fought back."

Dad sat on the dark brown bench in the room and pulled me onto his lap.

"I understand you were frustrated, but you're not supposed to fight. You know that."

"I'm sorry."

"What's the child's name?" Mom asked.

"Nicholas Johnson."

"We're setting up a meeting with him, his parents and the teacher."

"Please don't do that," I begged.

"We won't tolerate bullying."

"I will handle it," I pleaded.

"Okay, you get one chance," Dad warned.

"Now, your punishment. No cellphone for one week."

I sighed. I wanted to contest this, but I knew better than to argue with my Jamaican parents.

"I'm going to make dinner now. Please put your phone in our bedroom," Mom said.

"Yes Mom."

I ambled up our white, winding staircase and entered my parents' bedroom. As I placed the iPhone 13 on their desk, I heard the iMessage notification.

My best friend Fred had texted me.

I perched on the bed and opened the chat.

"Did you hear about Nicholas?"

"No."

"His parents were fighting outside of school."

"Unfortunate news."

"You and your big words, James lol."

Fred sent another message.

"Isn't that sad?"

"I guess. He's mean, why should we care?"

"Maybe he's mean because he goes through a lot at home."

"I don't know."

The smell of curried goat greeted me.

"Anyway, it's dinner time. I'll see you at school tomorrow. Oh, they're confiscating my phone."

"Confiscating?"

"It means they're taking it away."

"Why didn't you just say that? Lol"

I headed downstairs.

At the dinner table, I mixed the white rice in the curried gravy and told my parents about my day and the spelling bee contest coming up in the next four weeks.

"Every grade six student is participating. The winner will represent the school against other schools in Toronto."

"You don't seem excited," Dad noted.

I shrugged.

They looked at each other, then at me.

When I first learned of the bee, excitement flowed through my veins. But not anymore.

"Okay, let's play James Spells," Mom said excitedly. This was a game the three of us had been playing since I was younger. My parents are very smart people. They always instilled in me the importance of education, and they made learning fun.

First word," Dad said. "Sophisticated."

I laughed. "Dad, this is so easy."

"Spell it then," he laughed.

"S-O-P-H-I-S-T-I-C-A-T-E-D"

"Correct!"

"Next word," Mom said. "Encourage."

"Come on guys, where's the challenge?" I chuckled.

"E-N-C-O-U-R-A-G-E."

"Okay, here's the challenge now."

"Ravenous."

I dissected the word slowly.

Dad had a smirk on his face.

"Ravenous," I repeated.

"R-A-V-E-N-U-S?"

"Awww so close!" Mom said.

"It's R- A-V-E-N-O-U-S."

"Ah, I said. Noted."

We laughed because we knew that that would be the last time I'd spell that word wrong.

"You see the way your face lit up when we were playing?" Mom asked. "That's how I know there's more to the spelling bee than you are telling us."

Nicholas

"Stop throwing snowballs at us!" Jessica, my curly-haired red-headed classmate yelled. Her red beanie sat on her head covering her eyes. She looked at me angrily as tears stained her face.

Seeing her cry lit a fire inside me, thawing me out on the cold February morning. I grinned, picked up another round ball of ice and hurled it at her and her friends, Gabriela and Priya.

They screamed and scattered across the slippery school yard. Bored with taunting them, I went to the swings where several boys were playing marbles in the snow.

When Jerome, also Jamaican, saw me, his eyes bulged and his broad shoulders stiffened. He patted his friend Fred on the shoulder. Fred was a short, stocky boy who feared me. Jerome didn't though. I just knew I got on his nerves. Fred turned around and gasped, dropping his juice box. His freckles disappeared and were replaced by a pasty complexion.

"Please leave us alone," Fred said. His breath formed a perfect "O" in the wintery air.

"Or what?" I smirked.

"Why are you so obnoxious?" Jerome said.

"Why are you *obnocktus*?" I mocked.

"That's wrong." He rolled his eyes. I pushed him and he fell backwards.

"Leave us alone Nicholas!" Fred yelled, pushing me.

"You're so weak Fred. What kind of push was that?"

Suddenly, Jerome tackled me and the three of us wrestled in the middle of the school yard.

"You're like a bee! Always trying to sting us!" Jerome yelled as he punched me in the stomach. "Leave us alone." All the children egged us on. Ms. Brown and Mr. Mustafa ran to us. Mr. Mustafa held Jerome while Ms. Brown lifted me off Fred.

"Why are you fighting?" Ms. Brown asked.

We didn't answer. Just stared at each other, fuming.

"Detention after school! All of you!" Mr. Mustafa yelled.

We returned to our classroom. The shift from natural light to fluorescent lighting burned my eyes. I took my seat at the back of the class and listened to my peers. I overheard Janice and Alisha discussing how excited they were at the sleepover. Ramandeep and Tunde confirmed their plans to ride bikes home together after school. Jerome glared at me from across the room as Fred spoke to him.

I bit my nails. Everyone had a friend they were communicating with, except me. I'd been living in Canada for eight months and hadn't done great at settling in. Neither did my parents. They always fought, and my dad moved out after losing his job.

When I started Colehill Elementary School, kids teased me because of my accent. I became aggressive, taunted them and they stopped picking on me. They would either fear me or be my friend.

Ms. Brown waltzed into the classroom.

I liked her because she was nice to me. Other teachers treated me badly because I repeated sixth grade. I was supposed to be in seventh but had trouble reading and spelling. Ms. Brown always helped me with my work. She encouraged me by saying "You're not dumb. You can do anything you want to do." I didn't agree. My father told me that I was slow and would waste this opportunity in Canada.

"Settle down class," she said, as she stood on the platform.

"Today we have a pop quiz!"

We groaned.

I sunk in my seat, my heart racing.

Ms. Brown asked for a volunteer to hand out the quizzes. Jessica raised her hand. I glared at her as she put the papers on each desk. She was a teacher's pet. She glided around the room, smiling at everyone. Saving me for last, she placed the paper on my desk, her eyes fixed on her shoes the entire time. A small part of me felt bad she was afraid to look at me, but that part was quickly overtaken by an urge to make her even more terrified. I stuck my foot out as she walked away. She tripped over my ankle and stumbled, grabbing on to the brown, solid wood coat rack for support.

"Nicholas, why did you do that?!" she screamed.

"Ms. Brown, Nicholas tripped me on purpose!"

"It was an accident," I cried out.

Ms. Brown marched over to us.

"Nicholas, was it an accident?" she asked.

I nodded eagerly. "Yes, it was Ms. Brown."

In my peripheral, I saw Jessica roll her bright, hazel eyes.

"Tell her you're sorry, Nicholas."

"I'm sorry," I mumbled.

Ms. Brown patted Jessica gently on the head and directed her to her seat.

I grinned.

"You may begin," she said.

I turned my paper over, wrote my name and the date then read the first question.

"What is the homophone for stationary?"

I skipped it and read the second.

"Which one of these words is not a homonym?

a) Bear

b) Bark

c) Mean

d) Spring

e) Elephant

I skipped that as well and moved on. As I read each question, my palms sweated, and my heart raced. I didn't know the answers. I peered at my classmates who were writing on their papers. I put my head on the desk and took a nap. About twenty minutes passed and I heard Ms. Brown's soft voice.

"Pencils down, everyone."

She walked around the room and picked up our papers. When she got to me, she had a sad look on her face.

"Speak to me after class, Nicholas," she whispered, then walked to the front of the classroom.

"I have an announcement. Next month, we'll have our first annual spelling bee." My classmates chat among themselves eagerly as she went over the details.

"Everyone knows Jerome is going to win," Jessica said. The class nodded.

"Guys stop," Jerome said, pretending to be humble. He was a good speller. I bet his parents helped him with homework. Mine didn't care if I brushed my teeth before bed.

School ended and the three of us stayed behind in the classroom for detention. We cleaned the chalkboard, swept and mopped and threw out the garbage. While we did this, Ms. Brown marked the quiz papers. At the end, she asked Fred to wait outside while she spoke to Jerome and me.

"I don't know why you guys cannot get along," she said. "But you'll study for the bee together. Hopefully, you will learn that you have stuff in common."

I was happy Ms. Brown was forcing us to bond. I really wanted a friend, but my pride got in the way.

"I don't want to," I said.

"Neither do I," Jerome replied.

"You don't have a choice. If you don't you won't participate in the bee."

Jerome groaned. The spelling bee was a very big deal for him.

"Fine," he mumbled.

Inside, I felt excited. Maybe Jerome's smartness would rub off on me. Outside, I pretended that Ms. Brown had just done the worst possible thing to me.

Jerome

We laughed as Mom shared a joke about growing up in Jamaica. Since Ms. Brown told me I had to help him prepare for the bee, he and I hung out every day after school at my house. He sat across from me at the glass dining table. Dad was working late and was on his way home with pizza for dinner, after which he would drive Nick home. Mom sat with us, helping us prep for the bee tomorrow. Nick had made great progress, and we developed a friendship after working together for a month.

"Okay boys, break is over, back to spelling," she said through a final chuckle.

She gave Nick the word, "ambiguous" and he spelled it easily.

I gave him a high five. "See, you're not even stuttering anymore. You're going to do so great tomorrow!"

Nick's brown eyes glistened with pride. Mom and I exchanged smiles. It had been an interesting month. The first night he came over, he was so quiet. At first, I thought he was just pretending to be shy to fool my parents, but after an hour, I realized he genuinely wanted to learn. He was funny, too. We became friends quickly.

The garage door opened, announcing Dad's arrival.

"I'm going to help your father with the pizza," Mom said.

After she left, I asked Nick a question that had been on my mind.

"Why were you so mean to me and everyone at school?"

Nick played with his shirt nervously. "People made fun of me when I started Colehill, so I decided to fight back and then I just couldn't stop."

"I never made fun of you."

"No, you didn't. You were nice to me." He paused and then said, "I'm sorry."

"It's okay."

The smell of Dominoes' pizza greeted our noses before my parents entered the kitchen. Dad rubbed Nick's head the same way he greeted me. We ate dinner, joked around, and did a last-minute prep before Dad and I drove Nick home.

Nick lived in the co-operative housing complex just ten minutes from our house. When Dad turned onto Nick's street, we saw flashing lights. Two police cars were parked in front of his grey brick house. His mom, whom I had only seen once for a moment when Dad dropped him off, stood on their snow-covered lawn, angrily yelling at a man.

"What's going on here?" Dad mumbled.

He parked his car a few houses away from the house.

"James, stay in the car," Dad said sternly. "Nick, come, I'll take you to the house." I looked over at Nick, who was frozen beside me in the back seat.

"I don't want to go," he said.

"Dad, can Nick just stay with us for the night?"

"I don't know, son," Dad said as calmy as he could. After letting out a heavy sigh, dad exited the car and came around for Nick.

"It'll be okay," I said softly, patting him on the shoulder.

"Who is that man, Nick?" Dad asked when he opened the back door.

"My dad." "He moved out a few weeks ago because they were always fighting."

Dad helped Nicholas gather his things and slowly walked up to house. As they approached, the police threw Nick's dad on the lawn, handcuffed him, and put him in the back of one of the police vehicles. Nick's mother ran over to Nick and hugged him as he cried hysterically. She said something to Dad through tears, and they both headed inside.

"What happened?" I asked when Dad returned.

"I'm not sure, son," he said softly.

Our car ride home was quiet.

The spelling bee was set to start at 2:30 p.m., and at 2:15, Nick still hadn't arrived. At exactly 2:30, Nick walked in the auditorium, looking exhausted and disheveled. His clothes were wrinkled, his white sneakers covered in mud. He walked onto the stage and sat a few rows behind me. I tried to get his attention, but he kept his head down.

The bee started. One by one, each of the twenty children walked up to the microphone and spelled the words they were given. The words grew harder and harder until only five students remained. We kept going until we were down to the final two: Nick and me. I glanced over at him and I saw a mix of nerves and excitement on his face. He looked better than when he had first arrived.

It was my turn.

"Ravenous," the moderator said. I glanced at my parents, and we smiled. I looked at Nick who was looking at me, smiling. I had told him the story of that word. He knew I could spell it. I turned back to the audience.

"R-A-V-E-N-U-S."

The crowd "aww'd."

"Sorry, Jerome, that's incorrect."

I returned to my seat.

"Nicholas, you're up."

Overwhelmed by my generosity, Nick slowly approached the mic. If he spelled the word correctly, he would win. He looked at me, and I gave him a thumbs up.

"R-A-V-E-N-O-U-S."

The crowd cheered as the moderator announced that Nick was the winner of Colehill Elementary School's first annual spelling bee. I hugged him tightly.

"Congratulations!" I said. My parents ran up on the stage and hugged him.

"Why did you do that?" he asked.

I shrugged. "You deserve it," I smiled.

"Thank you for believing in me," he said through tears.

"I'm proud of you," Dad said as he rubbed my head. Mom nodded in agreement and gave me a big hug.

Hide and Tag

by Peter Tetteh Loveson

lick. Click. Click. Kyra lay still. She could hear her brother Kofi turning the lights on and off. Holding her breath, she listened, following his footsteps. "Ow!" he exclaimed. Kyra held back a giggle. "He is by the bed," she thought. He was always hitting his foot on the end of the bed. "I think I can..." Slowly raising her head from underneath the pile of blankets, she could see him through the slightly open closet door. He was moving towards her play corner. "I gotcha!" he shouted, pulling open the door on her princess castle.

"What? Ugh. How is she not here? She's always here."

Kyra chuckled quietly to herself. "You're not getting me today." Kofi stood up, crossed his arms, and looked around the room, a confused look on his face. All she needed was for him to turn around, and she could run from her hiding spot. But her brother was fast and always playing pranks on her. So maybe he knew she was hiding in the closet, but she couldn't move yet. All she had to do was make it to the living room and to their art table, and she would be safe. She was not going to let him win.

"You can do this, Kyra," she said to herself as she slowly began to move the blankets off of her, keeping an eye out for her brother. She saw Kofi as soon as she opened the closet door, a mischievous smile on his face. "Gotcha!" he yelled.

This was her chance. Throwing herself forward, Kyra screamed and ran to the bedroom door. Kofi was right behind her. "Oh, I'm gonna get you! Get back here!" Her heart pounded, racing so fast she thought it was going to fall out of her chest. She ran as fast as her legs could go. "Down the hall! Go legs, go! Move!" The thought of her brother catching her and winning the game made her run faster. But she was running too fast and crashed into the end of the hallway wall. Losing her balance, she stumbled back, but couldn't stop. Kofi was right behind her.

Kofi reached out to grab her. She moved her shoulder just in time and ran past him. She turned the corner, laughing and screaming, and could see their art table just past the couch. "Kyra!" Kofi was so fast. Kofi grabbed her arm.

"Yes, I'm safe!" She threw her fists in the air. Breathing heavily Kofi sat down, and placed his head on the table. He closed his eyes and took a couple of deep breaths. "How'd you get so fast?" he asked, still trying to figure out how he lost. Kyra laughed, dancing around her brother, excited she had finally won.

"You got lucky—I knew you were in there the whole time!" he argued.

"No, you didn't!" Kyra retorted, finally taking a seat next to him.

"Yes, I did," Kofi said, lifting his head off the table and staring at his sister. Kyra shrugged and smiled. "Well, you didn't get me," she said as she reached over and poked Kofi's arm. He didn't move. He just sat there, not moving, not saying a word. Kyra watched her brother and slowly moved her hand to poke Kofi again.

"Ahh!" he yelled as he jumped at her. Startled, Kyra jumped back in her chair. "Ay! Don't scare me like that. You made my heart scream."

Kofi burst out laughing, tilting his head. "How does your heart scream?"

Kyra looked at him. "It's a feeling. Like when I was running just now. I thought you were gonna catch me."

Kofi nodded. "Oh, okay. Do you want to play again? But I hide?"

Kyra's face lit up. She pushed her chair back and leaned into Kofi's face. "I'm gonna get you," she whispered in a low, deep voice.

"You won't find me," he smiled, taunting her. He slid out of his chair, stood up and scanned the room.

"Ready?" Kyra asked.

Kofi nodded, excited to find the best hiding spot—a new hiding spot. Kofi waited until Kyra was around the corner and started counting. "Five... Six... Seven..." Normally, he would hide somewhere in his room or their parents' closet, but this time he wanted to try the new couch. It was the perfect hiding spot with its oversized pillows and cushions, and he was small enough to lay behind them without revealing where he was.

He was pleased with his super cool new hiding spot, thinking how mad his sister was going to be when she couldn't find him. He was going to be the family's hide-and-tag champion.

"Eighteen... nineteen... twenty, ready or not, here I come!" Kyra's called out. Kofi closed his eyes and listened. He could hear her searching her room, and then his room. The whoosh of the shower curtain, followed by "I know you're here somewhere. I can smell you." Kofi let out a squeaky laugh. "Haha, you can't find me; I'm so smart."

Kyra walked down the hallway and into the living room. Then into the kitchen. Where she opened and closed all the cabinets.

"Kofi, I know you are here..." she sang as her footsteps stopped. Suddenly, Kofi had an itch on the left side of his shoulder. "No, no, no, I can't lose now." He tried to think about something—anything—to take his mind off the itch. "Pizza, chicken nuggets, ice cream..." But the itch didn't stop. He moved his left arm against the pillows, and for a few seconds, the itch went away, and then returned, worse. Just as he was about to reach over and scratch, he felt the couch move. He had forgotten about his sister!

"Oh no," he thought, "I can't make it to the art table in time." Kyra was close; it was now or never. He jumped from his hiding spot, catching his sister by surprise. He grabbed a pillow and used it as a shield to jump behind the couch. Kyra rushed forward, trying to grab him, but missed.

"Hey, no fair!" She squealed as she fell face first onto the couch.

"Ugh, how did you win again?!" Kyra whined as she sat up. She crossed her arms and looked across the room at Kofi laughing at the art table. Kofi scratched his shoulder. "Your face! You should see your face!"

This only made Kyra angrier. "You cheated; that's not fair!"

Kofi stopped laughing. "No, I didn't; I just used the pillow. That's not cheating!" He was so confused. How did he cheat?

He got up from the art table and started walking towards Kyra when she grabbed a pillow and ran straight at him, swinging it.

"I'm going to get you!" she growled. Kofi stood frozen, not sure what he should do. It was just a pillow, but Kyra was also really mad at him. Before he could do anything, Kyra hit him. He stumbled into the wall. Kyra shrieked with laughter, dropped the pillow, and ran. Kofi chased her.

"You're too slow," she teased as she turned the corner and slammed into the side of the hallway wall. She could feel his arms closing in on her. She shook off his grip and ran down the hall to her room, locking the door just as he crashed into it.

"Ow!" he exclaimed. Kyra sighed; she was safe. "Are you okay?" she asked. There was no reply.

"Kofi?"

"Hey, yeah, I'm okay, just my face hurts from the door." Kofi sighed and sat against his sister's door. He felt really embarrassed. How did she win twice? He slowly stood up and went to the bathroom across the hall, turned the light on and splashed water on his face. "Maybe that will help," he thought, drying his face on a towel.

He stood in the doorway, wondering what he should do next. His dad was working in his office down the hall. His sister was in her room singing a song from a princess movie.

Maybe he could go play some video games. As he walked to his room, he had an idea and headed to the living room. He grabbed the pillow his sister threw at him and climbed into his hiding spot in the couch, then placed the pillow in its spot. He was going to win, even if he had to wait. His mischievous smile was now hidden behind the pillows and cushions. He was going to win, and it felt good.

Kyra was sitting, playing video games on her TV. She was racing, and in 3rd place, about to reach 2nd but the mean spiky turtle kept getting in her way. "Ugh, move. I wanna win! No! Not again!" She rolled her eyes as her racer got hit and knocked off the track. "Ugh! Why won't you let me win!"

Her father knocked. Looking up, she exclaimed, "Papa!" He knelt down and kissed the top of her head. "Hey, Kyra, how are you?"

Kyra smiled shyly. "I'm good. How was work?"

Her dad sighed and smiled. "It was good; I'm happy to be done."

Kyra nodded. "Me too." Standing up, Kyra's dad, Samuel, looked at his watch. "Are you hungry for lunch? It's 12:30."

"Yes! Can we have chicken nuggets?" Kyra asked excitedly. Samuel laughed. "You love your chicken nuggets, don't you?"

Kyra started doing a ballet dance and singing, "Yes, they are the best!" Samuel watched his daughter dance. He loved her carefree spirit. She was so much like her mother.

"Okay, your majesty—let's go make chicken nuggets! Oh, where's your brother?" Kyra stopped dancing, and shrugged. "I don't know—we were playing hide and tag earlier, but I came to my room."

Samuel nodded. "Okay, I'll go find him." Samuel opened Kofi's door. "Kofi, you in here?"

He opened the closet door, but he wasn't in there. He looked under his bed, but he wasn't there either. Samuel sighed; Kofi was hiding; he was sure of it. He walked back to

Kyra's room. "Hey, come with me to the kitchen so we can make chicken nuggets, and then you tell me everything that happened with your brother."

Kyra told him everything. Sitting at the dining table, Samuel came up with a plan. He winked at Kyra, who smiled back, slightly confused, but she knew her dad had some good ideas. "Well, Kyra, after you eat, I'll count, and you hide." Samuel was impressed. Wherever Kofi was hiding, he was committed because he never missed lunchtime.

"Hmm. I guess Kofi is going to miss ice cream and cookies too." Kyra covered her mouth, trying to stifle her laugh, which sounded like a tire losing air. Samuel chuckled quietly as his daughter tried to hide her excitement.

"Okay, I'm done," Kyra said, taking her plate to the sink.

"Okay, let's do this," Samuel replied.

"Okay, let's do this," Kyra echoed, causing her dad to stick his tongue out and shake his head playfully.

"Okay, so count to twenty, and then come find us," Kyra instructed her dad. "That's how you play. Okay Papa?"

Samuel made a serious face and saluted Kyra. "Okay!" They both laughed. Samuel walked to his bedroom, pretending not to hear Kyra heading towards the bathroom. Samuel leaned against the bedroom door; he liked to wait before starting the count, adding to the surprise. He wished his wife was home. She always found the best hiding spots, so he knew where Kofi got it from.

"Okay, it's time to count. Ten... eleven... twelve..." Kyra moved from her hiding spot in the bathroom closet and sprinted down the hall to the kitchen, and hid behind some shopping bags under the sink, hoping her dad wouldn't search for her there. It seemed like such a good idea.

"Nineteen and three-quarters... twenty! Ready or not, here I come." Kyra held her breath as she heard her dad searching each room. "Are you here? Aw, you're not. Hmm, I wonder where she could be," she heard him say in a funny voice. He was always doing voices and making her and Kofi laugh.

She heard her dad walk past the couch as he hit it. "Hey, Kofi… where are you?"

"Hey, Kyra, where are you?" He searched the bathroom but he didn't find her there. "Wow, I guess the kids just turned into ghosts and disappeared," he said loudly. "I guess I have the house to myself until Mom gets home from work with pizza later."

Then Kyra heard his footsteps heading towards the bedroom hallway, so she tried sneaking out. The bags were loud, but maybe she'd get lucky and he wouldn't hear her. She crawled out from under the sink and quietly closed the door. The house was quiet. Too quiet.

Suddenly Samuel swung the door open. "Rawr, I got you!" Kyra ran around the counter and sped out of the kitchen.

"No, please, I give up—don't tag me!" she yelled and laughed as she tried to figure out where to go next. "Wait, wait, timeout. I need to drink water," she panted, grabbing her stomach.

Samuel laughed. "Okay, that's fine; I need a water break too... and I still haven't found your brother. I'm a little worried. But I think I'll go sit on the couch and relax for a bit."

Kyra giggled. "Yeah, the couch is so great." After they drank their water, Samuel gave the signal, and they both yelled and started throwing the pillows off the couch.

Kyra was shocked. Kofi was asleep behind the pillows and cushions. Samuel looked at his son. "Impressive. Hiding in the couch and falling asleep—that's a new one." "Should we wake him up, or just leave him alone?" Kyra asked.

Samuel put a gentle hand on her shoulder. "He'll be okay. I'll let him stay there for a bit, I'm just glad that we found him."

He didn't want to have to explain to his wife how he "lost" their son. He looked down at his watch. It was 2:00 p.m. It's still early, he thought. But yes, I really should wake up Kofi.

"Hey, Kofi, wake up, Kofi, wake up!" he shouted, huge smile on his face. Kofi opened his eyes, a little confused, and before he could say anything, his dad tapped his hand and ran away laughing.

"Tag, you're it, Kofi!"

Sunday Morning Mandir with a Big Pot of Dhal

by Saira Batasar-Johnie

All I could hear was Nani singing her morning bhajans in front of our altar. Nani didn't like coming to Canada because it was cold. She said the air dried out her skin. But her eldest daughter's birthday was special. My mommy was turning 40. Mommy invited all her siblings from New York and Guyana.

Divya and I stayed under the covers. We did not want to get out of bed. Amara opened the door and came inside our room and joined us.

"Are you ready for this weekend?" she asked. "The New Yorkers should be here soon. Nani made a whole spread of food."

Divya rolled over and moaned, "it's too early for curry."

"Oil roti, sada roti, pumpkin, katahar curry, fry chana, tomato choka, belanjay choka, and dhal and rice. This lady does not disappoint," Amara said, drooling. "She won't let me eat it until they come. I'm so hungry, and of course, Mommy sending me to hang out the laundry."

"Anjali, Divya, Mara Bara—wake up, my loves," Poowah Deepa called from the kitchen.

"It's Saturday. It should be illegal for us to wake up this early—8 a.m. is too early. Don't they know we need sleep to grow?" I groaned at Amara.

"If I have to wake up to clean, you two have to wake up, too." Amara took our sheets off.

Divya and I moseyed out of bed and to the washroom. We brushed our teeth, washed our faces and did a slow-mo walk to the kitchen.

Amara swiped an oil roti from Poowah and shared it with us. It was so fresh and warm, like a fluffy piece of heaven in my mouth. It would taste even better with some katahar.

Nani caught us eating.

"Wah all tree ah yuh ah do here?"

"Sita Ram, good morning, Nani," I said, giving her a big hug, hoping she wouldn't yell at me..

"Ram Ram, Sita Ram, Beti. The roti tastin' nice. Soon come your Mamoo Hardeo, Mamoo Krishna and cousins, then we will eat. Dem should be here in no time."

I was praying no time meant on time instead of GST (Guyanese Standard Time), as Mamoo Krishna would say.

***

The living room was filled with people, the kitchen bursting with smells that filled my tummy before I entered it. Divya ran wild with our cousins, Kumari, Trisha, and Shiva. Amara took the older girls to her room, while I watched my mom with her siblings and Nani. Reunited, sharing stories about

75

Guyana. Nani was happy; her children, whom she rarely saw, were finally with her. She kept touching Mamoo's face, telling my other Mamoo to keep eating. It had been five years since they had seen Nani.

Poowah Deepa called us into the kitchen. It was time for Operation Decorate the Mandir for Mommy's birthday. She assigned us each a task and a bag. Poowah had organized with Pandit Ramlall for us to decorate the Mandir on Saturday evening after all the functions. We were so excited we each had a special task to work on to make this day extra special for Mommy. But first, I had to eat.

Poowah and Mami Meena took out our food and we all sat together. Everyone got a bowl of dhal with oil roti and katahar, pumpkin and tomato choka—all the things that were my favourite.

We ate, had seconds and thirds until there was no more room to eat. Nani sat with us and watched.

"It tasting nice?" Meh gah teach all yuh pikney tomorrow marnin'. Abeedese must wake up early and help Nani cook for the Mandir. We will make a special menu for yuh muddah," Nani said.

Everyone groaned, but I was excited. I loved Nani's food and I was finally going to have a chance to watch her cook.

We hurried along and washed up. Poowah told my mom she was taking us out for ice cream and to Patsy's Bakery Shop down the road, but it was Operation Decorate Mandir time.

"So we aren't really getting ice cream?" Shiva asked.

"We will get a treat after Mandir. We did tell her we are going out for ice cream, so if we come home empty-handed, she will give us her mom eyes," Poowah replied.

We all laughed. My mom was known for her mom eyes. It's that look that conveys you're doing something you know that you shouldn't, but you are doing it anyway. And when my mommy catches you, you freeze and slowly stop and back away, and then she makes "mmmhmmm" sounds. She was the Mausi to everyone that you did not want to vex up, but also the Mausi that would fill your belly with anything your heart desires. My mom was known for her khurma. She made the best khurma because her Nani taught her how to make it.

"We are here!"

Eight of us got out of the van, unloaded, and got to work. The big kids were in charge of the centrepieces and flower decorations. The little kids were in charge of the streamers and balloons. Poowah put bhajans on while we decorated, and we used all of Mommy's favourite colours—purple, yellow, and orange—throughout the Mandir. Poowah dressed the deities with new outfits, preparing them in lilac purple lehenghas and kurtas.

When we were done, we went to Patsy's Bakery Shop. They had my favourite ice cream there—coconut cream. Amara ordered mango and coconut, Shiva ordered guava, Poowah ordered soursop, and my other cousins got passion fruit and a mix of coconut and mango. Poowah ordered a tub of coconut and mango ice cream to take home.

When we got home, Mami Meena was making khurma with my mom. The house smelled sweet. They began working on the bags to share after the puja. Nani brought special purple bags with a gold Om from Guyana for Mommy. We all got to work. My Mamoos were outside peeling and chopping up pumpkin, aloo and katahar. My Mami Sabi was washing bhaji in the sink.

77

Nani called me over, "Anju, meh gah teach yuh fah mek dhal, my special dhal. Go and wash up yuh hand."

"Okay, Nani."

Babla and Kanchan played in the background—my Mamoos always had the best chutney songs.

Nani took out a big bag of yellow split peas, with two big silver basins. She told me to keep throwing in the dhal, as if my hands were measuring cups."

She told me to fetch hot water to pour into the bowls. She mixed the dhal and took out the bad pieces. She covered the bowls with tea towels and said we'll cut everything fresh in the morning.

"Chilren, goo and bade and catch yuh bed," Nani yelled.

Shiva brought a flashlight and we made different shadow figures on the ceiling. Amara and Arianna told us scary stories, and I dozed off.

***

I awoke to the Hanuman Chalisa playing in the kitchen. I tip-toed around my cousins as they slept, freshened up and went to meet Nani who was chopping fresh cilantro and parsley.

"Anju, yuh wake up early," Nani said with a bright smile. I could see her gold teeth shining through.

"Nani, you said you would teach me to make your dhal. I want to help make it for Mommy; she loves your dhal," I told her.

"Leh we get to wuk den." Nani tied an apron around me.

She showed me how to clean the dhal, how to rinse, and rinse, and rinse more until the water was clear.

Nani had a special way of cooking her dhal. I watched as she put the oil in the big karahi, then the dhal.

"Pass me de grind jeera." She sprinkled it all over.

"Nani, how do you know how much to put in the pot?"

"Yuh must average, and yuh gah know." I looked at her, puzzled, and said "okay."

She continued to sprinkle salt, black pepper and turmeric into the pot of yellow split peas and fried it up.

She added boiling water from the kettle twice and turned the dhal, and she asked me to turn it with her while she hummed a bhajan. We left it to boil.

I washed four wiri wiri peppers, chopped up bhaji and began working on the other items on the menu. Nani put me to sit on a stool with a piece of puri to eat. My Mami's were cooking outside and I watched as they all laughed and sung. The creation of the food for the Mandir was made with so much love for my mommy.

Nani told me to add the bhaji. I watched as she mashed and mixed it with the long stick.

The dhal was almost done.

"Pass me the big jeera, Anju." She put oil in the ladle, added the whole pieces of jeera, and put it over a burner. "Dis is wah we does call chowkay." Once the jeera began getting darker, she put in the dhal and covered the pot. After one minute, we opened the pot of dhal.

"Anju, you stir de pot." I stood on the chair, held the pot with an oversized oven glove and began to stir. My Nani stood behind me and held my hand. She put her cheek on my cheek, "Anju, yuh did the best job mekin the dhal for yuh mommy." The aroma of the dhal filled the house, waking everyone, and soon there was a mad dash as we scrambled to get dressed for the Mandir.

Everyone helped everyone get dressed. Mami tied the sarees, and Mommy helped with our lehenghas. Daddy-ji came home from work and helped the Mamoos put the food in the cars.

Nani had our bindis and bangles; she put one on each of our foreheads and found matching bangles for our outfits. I watched Mommy and her sisters-in-laws put on their make-up, eye shadow and blush everywhere.

***

At the Mandir, everyone helped take things inside. Poowah had given us our jobs the night before:

"Box of puja items...Shiva, take it to the pandit. All the sweet bags—Amara and Arianna, take them to the back. Anju, Trisha, take the flowers to the front and tell the pandit they are already washed."

I watched my Mamoos lift the big pot of dhal and carry it carefully to the kitchen.

We all settled into our spots at the front of the Mandir and watched as others arrived with gifts and flowers. Mommy was well-known. She participated in the Mandir every week and ran the children's group.

"Om, He Heramba Tvamehyehi
Hyambikatryambakatmaja,

80

Siddhi-Buddhi Pate Tryaksha Lakshalabha Pituh Pitah,

Nagasyam Nagaharam Tvam Ganarajam Chaturbhujam,

Bhushitam Svayudhaudavyaih Pashankushaparashvadhaih,

Avahayami Pujartham Rakshartham Cha Mam Kritoh,

Ihagatya Grihana Tvam Pujam Yagam Cha Raksha Me,

Om Siddhi-Buddhi Sahitaya Shir Mahaganadhipataye Namah

Avahayami-Sthapayami."

The Pandit blew through a conch shell. We sat behind Mommy while she performed the puja. Pandit Ramlall gave Mommy a gold plate called a tharia with a diya and flower petals all around it. We all stood up and held the right arm of the person in front of us.

We walked in a line and did aarti of all the deities. Amara and I gave each deity an envelope with money.

We then proceeded to Nani and performed aarti on her, and she put her right hand up, with her palm facing us. Mommy put a flower on her head, took the tharia and circled it around her face three times and then we bowed to her feet for blessings. Nani touched our heads and then we gave her a group hug. Nani and Mommy both cried and smiled. We did the same to other older people at the Mandir. Following this, everyone began performing aarti to the deities and the elders. Some people came to my mom and performed aarti on her.

Poowah Deepa called for me and Amara to fetch the cake. We gave our jobs to our other Mandir cousins and went to the kitchen.

Daddy-ji asked the singers to sing the Baar Baar birthday song, a classic that we play for everyone's birthday.

Baar baar din ye aaye

Baar baar dil ye gaaye

Tu jiye hazaaron saal

Ye meri hai aarzoo

Happy Birthday to you

Happy Birthday to you

Happy Birthday to, Aunty Seeta

Happy Birthday to you

We took pictures as a family, with everyone who came from New York and Nani. We fed Mommy and her brothers put cake on her face. It was time to serve the dhal that we made. The other Mandir aunties were already in the kitchen preparing everything; however, my Nani told them not to touch the dhal.

The first plate of food we made was for Pandit Ramlall. Then we fed the singers of the kirtan group. I walked around with my Nani and poured dhal into everyone's plate who wished to try it.

Mommy had a plate of plain rice and roti on the side, and she waited patiently for us to arrive. I poured the dhal on her rice, this golden liquid, a taste of home and tradition, that filled our tummies with comfort. She closed her eyes as if the flavours transported her from the earth. When she swallowed, she stood up and gave Nani a hug.

"No, Seeta, must give Anju the kiss. She was the main cook."

My Mommy looked at me and kneeled.

"I am so proud of you Anju. You made it taste just like home."

She hugged me tightly, then sat down and told everyone in the Mandir to eat the dhal: "Anju mek it."

Nani and I watched as everyone ate. "I now understand what Poowah means when she says, 'I made it with love'—the feeling of cooking something with our hands and sharing it with everyone."

Nani and I truly made the big pot of dhal with love.

Glossary

Abeedese – Everyone, all of us

Aloo – Potato

Belanjay – Eggplant

Bindi – Middle of forehead sticker

Bhaji – Spinach

Chana – Chickpeas

Chowkay - Frying up jeera and garlic

Diya - Oil lamp

Karahi – Big silver cooking pot

Katahar – Jackfruit or breadnut

Khurma – A sweet dish

Lota - Gold cup used in prayers

Mandir – Hindu temple

Mami – Mother's brother's wife

Mamoo – Mother's brother

Mausi – Mother's sister

Nani – Mother's mom

Poowah – Father's Sister

Puja – Prayers

Puri – Deep-fried roti

Tharia – Gold plate used in prayers, also known as Thali

Joey's Not a Basketball Pro

by Abigail Grimes

Joey sat in the bleachers watching her sister run up and down the basketball court. She was incredibly fast and could jump very high. Joey would be on her feet, cheering louder than anyone when Sabrina scored. She was Sabrina's personal pep squad.

Joey's mom made sure they were early to get good seats, so Sabrina could see them cheering her on. The gym was packed.

Sabrina's team, the Jaguars, was playing their rival team, the Panthers, in the semi-finals to decide who would face the Grizzlies in the finals.

The last seconds were ticking down in the fourth quarter, with the game tied 20-20.

Everyone watched the shot clock as the kids raced across the court.

Suddenly, the referee blew his whistle loudly and called a foul.

A hush fell over the crowd as Sabrina walked to the free throw line. Joey grabbed her mom's hand and leaned forward in her chair.

As Sabrina bounced the ball, Joey held her breath. She took the shot and it sailed into the basket. The referee caught it and passed it back.

Sabrina bounced the ball, looked over at Joey and their mom and winked. Joey giggled and winked back.

Sabrina made her second shot, and Joey watched as the ball appeared to move in slow motion toward the net. It bounced off the backboard, circling the rim again and again, before finally dropping in.

Joey jumped out her seat and pumped her fists in the air. The gym erupted with cheers.

The Jaguars won! They were set to face the Grizzlies the following week!

The team left the court to thunderous applause as the coach offered to take them out for pizza.

Sabrina emerged from the changeroom, hugged Joey and her mom, then joined her team as they rushed across the street to the local pizza parlour.

Joey watched her sister and wondered if, maybe one day, she would be good enough to join the team, help them to victory, and enjoy celebratory pizza afterward.

The next day at school, Sabrina was treated like a hero. Joey was so proud of her big sister. Being two grades behind, she looked up to her.

Joey felt like a newcomer at school. She had graduated from Grade 5, and now, in sixth grade, she was a senior. They had a homeroom, lockers, and moved from class to class. It was a big change, but Joey felt okay about it because her big sister was there, and at least they still got recess. The biggest change was the new teachers. Joey's favourite teacher was Mr. Cooke, who had been Sabrina's gym teacher and was now hers.

"Aren't you Sabrina's sister?" Mr. Cooke asked.

"Yes, I am!" Joey said with pride.

"Oh, well then you must also be good at basketball. We'll make you center. You can do the tip-off for your team," Mr. Cooke said, nodding intently.

The class was divided into two teams, and although Joey wasn't the tallest kid, she took her position in the centre of the court.

Joey looked at the bench—her usual spot. It was close to the action, but not too close. A place where she could cheer or scowl at the ref like the pros did on TV.. Besides being in the stands with her mom, the bench was Joey's favourite place.

"Ummm, Mr. Cooke," Joey said, nervous about being at the centre of the action.

Joey looked at the other team's center. Peter Jenkins had been in her class since kindergarten, but they hadn't started hanging out until Grade 3, when Joey developed an interest in marbles. Peter was always in the schoolyard digging marble pits with the heel of his sneakers, or laying flat on his belly with his tongue sticking out and one eye closed, as he lined up the perfect shot.

Peter had that same look of concentration on the court and Joey felt butterflies in her stomach.

Mr. Cooke bounced the ball between Peter and Joey, then held it at their eye level. Peter smiled at Joey, then looked up at the ball in anticipation.

"Mr. Cooke?" Joey called again. She must not have said it loud enough, because the next thing she knew, Mr. Cooke had blown the whistle and tossed the ball high in the air.

Peter jumped and swatted his hand at the ball, but he missed. Joey jumped too and it grazed her fingertips. They looked at each other and laughed, then everyone raced after the ball as it bounced down the court. Mr. Cooke shouted encouragement, knowing everyone was trying their best. Joey jumped, dribbled, and chased her classmates. It was fun, but she didn't think she was playing basketball—certainly not the way her sister had the night before.

Every time someone passed the ball to Joey, Mr. Cooke watched with anticipation. As the game went on, that look shifted to disappointment. Joey loved watching the basketball float through the air and swish through the net. She had seen her sister do it a hundred times and wished she could do the same.

Then, with seconds to go, she had the ball in her possession. Before she could shoot, Tamara charged into her. The ball flew out of her hands and she landed on her butt on the floor.

TWEET!

Mr. Cooke blew the whistle. "Foul," he called and pointed to Joey, then thrust his thumb toward the foul line.

Joey gulped. The pressure was on!

The score was 12 to 10, and Peter's team was winning. Even worse, gym class was almost over. The best they could hope for was a tie.

"Come on, Joey!" "You can do it!"

Joey walked to the foul line and Mr. Cooke handed her the ball.

This must have been what it felt like for Sabrina yesterday. Except, she is actually good at basketball.

Joey exhaled deeply and bounced the ball. She looked up at the basket, then at the line, and exhaled.

She could hear the gymnasium clock tick between each bounce. The class was silent.

Her first shot ricocheted off the backboard and dropped cleanly through the net. Joey's team shouted with joy. Even Peter was smiling.

"Wow!" Joey exclaimed.

Mr. Cooke blew the whistle again and the teams settled down. She bounced the ball and took the shot.

BONK!

The ball hit the rim and sailed over Joey's head.

Everyone turned and looked at Joey, who watched, disappointed, as the ball rolled out of bounds on the other side of the gym. Peter's team shouted in celebration —they won the game, 12-11!

Mr. Cooke brought the whistle to his lips, but the school bell rang before he could blow it. Class was over and one thing was clear: Joey MacMillian was no basketball pro. Joey frowned and sat on the ground, looking up at the hoop. Why can't I do this? It's in my blood, isn't it?

That afternoon, during recess, Joey sat on the swings and watched Peter grind his heel into the dirt to make a fresh marble pit.

"Wanna play?" Peter asked.

"Why? So I can suck at that, too?"

"You're great at marbles!" Peter laughed. "Let's play."

Peter pulled out a blue velvet bag containing his favourite marbles. He fished out a big blue one with gold flecks resembling stars.

Joey had always admired that one. When she went to the store to get new marbles, none of the packs ever had it.

"If you weren't good, I wouldn't be nervous to play you. I could lose my blue galaxy."

"You wanna play keepsies?" Joey asked, raising her eyebrow and pointing at the star-studded marble in Peter's hand.

"Yep." Peter smiled. "The swing set and the grass are out of bounds."

Joey climbed off the swings and took her marbles out of her pocket. She didn't have a fancy velvet bag like Peter. She kept hers in a resealable bag that, a month ago, had a bologna sandwich in it.

"You have to let it go. It's just gym."

"To you it's just gym. But to me—Sabrina's sister? It's a lot of pressure. It's supposed to be natural. I'm just supposed to be good at it, you know?"

"I guess," Peter said.

Joey shrugged and lay on the ground to get a good look at the marble pit Peter designed. She looked up and nodded her approval.

They pulled out their aggies, turned the bags upside down, scattering the marbles within the boundaries of the game. Then they took ten steps back and began to play.

Their game packed as much drama and suspense as could fit into a fifteen-minute recess.

Peter sunk two of Joey's boulders with one shot.

"Lucky shot!" Joey called out. She leaned against the swing set watching Peter's moves, waiting for him to miss.

"It's not luck, it's skill," he laughed. "Just like it's not luck that you were the only one who got an A on Ms. Pingle's spelling test."

Peter crouched over the marbles and moved his head from side to side. Joey thought he looked like a bird when he did that.

"Oh, that was easy!" Joey laughed.

"For you, maybe."

"Well, to be honest, my mom quizzed me every night for a week!"

Peter lined up his shot, and sunk Joey's aggie.

"Oh, man!"

"Better luck next time," Peter chuckled and scooped up the marbles in the pit.

He pulled the bag from his pocket and put the smaller marbles away. Then, he picked up the two boulders, swirling them in his hand to remove the dirt. Joey's silver marble looked really cool beside his galaxy speckled one.

Joey watched with a hint of sourness as Peter placed the two fancy marbles into the sack and tied it.

"Next time, for sure! I'm gonna win back my boulder and I'm going to win that blue galaxy!" Joey said.

The bell rang and Joey put her remaining marbles in the sandwich bag.

Back in their homeroom, they waited at their desks for the afternoon lesson. On Tuesdays after recess, the Grade 1 class joined their reading buddies for story time. The first graders were thrilled to hang out with the big kids, and the big kids remembered how much fun it was to go down the hall and see the Grade 6 classroom.

This week, Joey and her buddy Tim, and Peter and his buddy Linda, were scheduled to go to the library. "Joey," Ms. Pingle called. "Make sure everyone goes directly to the library and let the librarian know you are there once you arrive."

"Yes, Ms. Pingle," Joey answered, with a big smile.

Ms. Pingle usually walked the students to the library, even though it was only just down the hall.

It meant a lot that Ms. Pingle trusted her to lead the group.

"Good afternoon, Mrs. Phillip," Joey said to the librarian.

"Good afternoon, children," came Mrs. Phillip's warm greeting.

"Is it Reading Buddy, day?"

"We're going to find some books and sit in the corner by the clock," Joey answered.

The library was Joey's favourite room in the school. It was filled with books about adventures, heroes and villains, and even cool recipes her mom let her try. She spent as much time there as her mom and teachers would allow.

She particularly enjoyed sitting on the soft blue carpet dotted with large yellow stars and crescent moons. It reminded her of Peter's blue galaxy marble.

Joey felt at home in the library and imagined Sabrina felt the same way about the gym.

Joey and Peter led their buddies to the primary section to choose books.

"We're going to read over by the cushions," Peter said.

"Okay, we'll go to the chairs," Joey replied.

"Can I read first?" Tim asked, his cheeks round and rosy as he looked up at Joey. "I've been practicing!"

"Of course!" Joey said and climbed into the chair to listen to Tim read.

Joey smiled and waited patiently as Tim sounded out difficult words. She only jumped in to help when asked. She could tell he had worked hard to improve.

Tim's story was about a kid named Jamal who tried out for the basketball team. He failed to make it the first time, but he kept trying. With perseverance and determination, Jamal eventually made the team and went on to help win the championship.

It reminded her of Sabrina's game-winning goal the other night, and her miserable performance earlier that day.

Joey smiled at Tim, who was beaming with pride.

"Wow, Tim!" Joey exclaimed. "You did such a great job! You're a pro at this!"

"I practiced and practiced. I wanted to show you I could do it all by myself!"

"You sure did!" Joey gave Tim a high five. "You're a superstar! Like you scored the game-winning basket!"

"I'm so glad I'm your buddy!" Tim said and hugged her.

"I'd say this is better than any basketball score," Joey said.

Joey spotted Sabrina in the library and felt a guilty flutter in her belly.

Sabrina walked over and tousled Joey's hair.

"What was that about basketball?" Sabrina asked playfully.

"Nothing," Joey mumbled.

"Joey, we're all good at something. So what if basketball isn't your thing? You're awesome at spelling and reading. You're super patient, and you're a great friend. You don't need to be good at basketball if you don't like it. I know that if you want to be good at something, nothing stops you from learning how to do it. That's what I admire most about you."

"Yep," Tim chimed in. "You're awesome."

"You're one of the coolest kids I know, and I'm not saying that because you're my sister," Sabrina stated.

"It's true!" Peter exclaimed. He had overheard Joey's conversation and had made his way over to the couch.

Joey trusted Sabrina, and if she said it didn't matter that she wasn't good at basketball —and if she wanted to be good at it, she would just have to practise —Joey believed her.

Joey thought about it for a moment and knew she didn't want to practice basketball anymore. She would rather watch Sabrina play and spend her time reading amazing adventures about far off places.

"Sabrina, you're right. I'm no basketball pro. I'm good at a bunch of other things."

Joey and Peter tidied up while their buddies stacked the books on the cart in front of Mrs. Phillip's big oak desk. Waving to Mrs. Phillip, the kids walked out of the library.

Sabrina headed back to her class on the first floor, and Joey and Peter walked their buddies back to their classroom. When the bell rang, Sabrina was waiting for Joey by the big rock in front of the school and they walked home together.

Joey ran up the steps to their townhouse and burst through the door.

"Hi Mom!" Joey called from the foyer as she untied her shoes.

Mom turned and smiled. "Hi kids! I just sliced up a mango. Would you like some?"

"Yes, please," Sabrina replied and entered the kitchen.

Sabrina and Joey washed their hands at the sink and then grabbed Mom into a big hug.

Sabrina scooped a few slices of fruit, then disappeared to watch TV.

"How was your day, Joey? Anything interesting happen?" Mom asked.

"Well, I tried to play basketball today. It was so embarrassing, Mom! I suck! Aren't I supposed to be good at it? Like Sabrina?"

"Don't say that." Mom gave her a gentle squeeze.

"I suck at basketball, and I lost my steel boulder to Peter in marbles," Joey sighed.

"How did the spelling test go?" Mom asked.

Joey sat up a bit, a small smile crossing her lips. "It went okay, I guess."

"You guess? Your teacher's email said you got an A. You should be proud of your accomplishments. I know I'm very proud of you!"

"Yeah, I got an A. I also spent time with my reading buddy. He hardly needed my help. I'm really proud of him!"

"You see, just like Sabrina's good at basketball, you're good at reading and spelling. You both work hard and you see great results from the effort you put in," Mom explained.

"It's okay I'm not great at basketball. It's not my thing. It's Sabrina's thing." Joey popped one more slice of mango into her mouth and got up from the table. She gave her mom a big, sticky kiss on the cheek. "Thanks, Mom!"

"Ugh!" Mom exclaimed with a chuckle. "You're welcome, Sweetheart."

Joey turned to head to the basement to watch TV.

"Have fun, but before you go, please toss those jeans in the wash," Mom directed.

"Yes, Mom!" Joey laughed and headed to her room to change her clothes.

Deciding TV could wait, Joey closed her door, picked up a book, and spent the rest of the afternoon lost in a story.

A Yearlong Visit to Grandma's House

by Ndija Anderson-Yantha

W e're going to Grandma's for a week," Mom says, tossing more clothes into the suitcase. I think it is odd that she is planning a trip to Grandma's out of nowhere—and that Dad is not coming—but I go along with the plan. However, it doesn't seem like there is an actual plan. All I know is that Dad went out earlier, and now Mom, who would normally put a great deal of thought into how close my strawberries were to my sandwich in my bento box, is grabbing shirts, socks, and shorts from the drawer and throwing them frantically into a suitcase.

"Should I pack my backpack too?" I ask, perplexed. "Bring whatever you think will make you comfortable, Cayden," she responds.

We put the bags in Mom's car. I'm excited but nervous. I had never stayed over at Grandma's for more than a couple of days at a time; but whenever I did, it was always great. During the holidays, Grandma always made my favourite meals, like cook-up rice and pepperpot. And nobody can make a better cup of tea! Drinking Grandma's orange pekoe tea was like getting a hug from inside out.

We exit the car in Grandma's driveway and the air almost suffocates me. It's muggy and the sweat on my skin has nowhere to go, but I'll take it over snow any day. I squeeze my pillow as I head toward the door. As I turn the handle, the warm smell of curry floats into my nose, and I know that dinner tonight is going to bless me.

Grandma greets me with a warm hug. "Yuh hungry?" she asks. "Even if I wasn't, the way it's smelling, I'm definitely eating!" I say, as I dashed to the kitchen table.

Just as I'm about to use my last piece of roti to wipe the curry clean from my plate, someone yoinks the flatbread from my grip.

"Mmmm, don't you just love Grandma's roti?" Kara says, as she pops it into her mouth. I didn't even hear when she came in.

"That's messed up, Kara! How are you gonna take my last piece of roti?"

"You snooze, you lose, Cous!"

Kara, my "sister-cousin," is my oldest and closest friend. She's just a year older than me, so we've always done everything together. Her mom is my mom's older sister. And since my parents never got around to having another kid, Kara is as close to a sibling as I'm ever going to get. Tonight, she's over at Grandma's house because my aunt wanted to check up on Mom.

"You two head upstairs; it's time for big-people talk," Grandma shouts from the laundry room. Kara and I reluctantly leave the kitchen and head to Mom's old room, where I would be crashing for the week. Kara pulls out her tablet and we scroll through reels on Mom's old twin bed until Auntie calls her to go home.

That night, I dream of my parents arguing. In the dream, I grab my pillow and head to the closet, where I curl up on the floor, imagining that it's a secret bunker where no one can find me. I put the pillow over my head to drown out their voices, but it doesn't work.

"Please, just stop!" I scream. "Just stop! Don't you know that if you don't stop, we're going to end up at Grandma's house! Could you please just stop? Please"

"Cayden. Cayden. Cayden! Wake up, you're having a bad dream!" I jump out of my sleep, to Mom sitting next to me on the side of the bed.

"You're safe, my love, you're safe," she reassures me, cradling my face in her hands.

"Mom, when are we going home?" I ask.

"Let's give it a couple of weeks for things to cool off," she replies. She kisses my forehead and leaves the room.

Eek, eek, eek, the grass squeaks under my Nikes as I hustle across the wet field to my new school. I can't believe that I'm at a new school. Mom's "couple of weeks" of cooling off at Grandma's turned into a couple of months. I had always looked forward to the first day of school—a new outfit, new school supplies, and another chance to make my parents proud. Not this year. Nothing feels right. Not even my new running shoes, even though they fit perfectly. I didn't get to buy them with Dad, which was always part of the fun.

Mom keeps telling me how "good" this school is, but I don't care, I don't want to go, and this is why I'm late. As I approach the school, every step brings on more dread. I don't know anybody here. My friends and I had been looking forward to starting fifth grade—friends from my old neighborhood, now living two towns over. We had been in the same class since junior kindergarten, and now I have to try and meet new people? What's Mom thinking? Doesn't she realize how hard all these changes are for me—especially without Dad or any friends to talk to? Doesn't she realize that I'm going to miss my chance to finally play intermediate soccer as a Steeplechase Public School Stallion? Doesn't she care about how I feel?

For the rest of the day, I just go through the motions. The first day wasn't as bad as I thought it was going to be, but it wasn't great either. My home room teacher made me stand up and introduce myself to the class, which was horrifying, and now I'm officially labelled as "The New Kid."

When I get home, I mutter "Good afternoon" to Grandma, and head upstairs. She can tell I don't feel like talking, so she doesn't stop me. I'm glad Mom isn't back from the office yet because I'm not ready to see her. I'm not happy. I mean, I get it—Mom and Dad don't get along, but now I'm the one who has to deal with the mess they've made.

I miss having Dad around. I miss my friends. I miss my room. I miss my bed. I miss our old house. When are we going back? Are we ever going back? I'm not sure what the plan is, or if there's even one at all, and none of the adults are giving me answers to my questions. I'm trying my best not to ask Mom all the time, but I think I deserve to know the timeline. I wonder if she'll ever tell me.

As the fall term goes on, I join a few clubs and, most importantly, I make the soccer team! I start making friends and getting into a routine. I also start spending time with Dad on Saturdays. He takes me to my swimming lessons, we go out for lunch, but I never stay over with him at our old place. I don't like going there without Mom anyway. It doesn't feel right.

When my parents see each other during those Saturday hand-offs, they barely speak. I'm still trying to figure out who these two people are, and what they have done with my mom and dad. Before Mom and I went to Grandma's, my parents argued a lot, but I also remember when they used to enjoy each other's company, watching movies together, going on road trips, visiting cool places like the Aquarium or the Science Centre, or just taking a walk in our neighbourhood. I miss how they used to look at each other with love. I miss us.

It seems like they have forgotten what things were like before and what they meant to each other. Maybe there is some way that Kara and I can help them to remember.

The snow is here now, and everything is either frozen or freezing, including me. Some days, it's hard to get out of bed. I keep dreaming of the day when I will wake up and we're back in our old house.

School eventually wraps up for winter break. Not too long ago, Kara, her little sister, Tia, and I helped Grandma decorate her tree, dancing to the cheery sounds of parang, sipping from our special batch of non-alcoholic sorrel, and eating black cake—a family tradition. We're all excited about the presents, but what I really want for Christmas is for my parents to get back together, so we can go back to our old life.

On Christmas Day, Dad comes over to Grandma's house to deliver my gifts and watch me open them. I used to love Christmas Day—exchanging gifts, the smiles and funny stories. Now Mom and Dad mostly exchange chilly glances, and are doing a pretty bad job at hiding how they feel about each other. Whenever they do manage to force a smile, it reminds me of the grimace of the pit bull owned by my old neighbour, Mr. Singh. I know they are trying to make the holidays memorable; but it's obvious they would be somewhere else if they had a choice. I'm actually glad when Dad leaves because so does the tension.

The coldest winter of my life melts into a spring of possibilities. As the months go on, it feels like my parents are settling into a new rhythm, becoming a bit more pleasant. I start getting hopeful about them getting back together.

One afternoon after school, Kara and I are scrolling through reels and come across the "Yes Day Challenge" where parents agree to say "yes" to everything their children request for a whole day. Suddenly, I have the most stellar idea: "Kara, I think we might be able to get my parents back together by doing the "Yes Day Challenge!"

"Cayden, you can't expect that your parents will just say "yes" to getting back together, just because you tell them to. It kinda doesn't work like that."

"No, no, I know that! That's not what I mean. We are going to get them to say "yes" to spending time together, like, on a date, but without them knowing they're going on a date."

I'm not sure how we are going to pull it off, but if we could get Mom and Dad to say "yes" to sitting together at the same table, then they would have no choice but to look into each other's eyes, and maybe they will remember how much they loved each other and try to work things out.

"Kara, this is going to be tricky, but I think we can make it happen."

"What's something you want me to know or want to ask me?" Mom asks me this question every night before I head to bed, then inquire about my favourite part of the day and what I might be excited for tomorrow. Most nights, I don't have much of a response, but tonight, I did:

"Mom, I was wondering if we could do the Yes Day Challenge?"

"The Yes Day Challenge?"

"Yes, the Yes Day Challenge. It's the one where you have to say "yes" to anything that I ask for 24 hours. All of my friends are making their parents do it? Could we do it too, pleeeease?" I say to her with begging eyes.

"Ummm…okay…sure," she says hesitantly. "When would you like to do it?"

"This Saturday, please!"

"Wow, that's quick, lemme see," she says, as she scrolls through the calendar app on her phone. "Sure, I think we can make that work," she says. "One thing though, do we have to post it on social media?"

"Mom, if it's not posted on the socials, does it even exist?"

"You're right, kiddo. We can post it on social media…I guess…" she relents.

I call Dad on video chat and ask him if he would be willing to meet me and Kara at the park for a picnic on Saturday afternoon at 1:00 p.m. He says "yes" without hesitation. My parents and I used to love going for picnics, sometimes in our own backyard. We made tuna sandwiches with mayonnaise, black pepper and green onion, and also pack snacks like chocolate chip cookies, ketchup chips, and gummy worms for our outdoor feasts. Hopefully, this picnic will help bring back those good memories.

I'm up super-early on the morning of my Yes Saturday. I can barely contain my excitement. I smell Grandma's bacon, my favourite! I rush to the kitchen, to Grandma in her floral house dress, frying the good stuff at the stove, and Mom, dressed and ready to go, helping herself to a cup of coffee.

"Morning, Grandma! Morning, Mom! Grandma, it's Yes Day!" I proclaim, as I take my seat at the table.

Grandma looks over her shoulder to greet me: "Yes, chile, morning! I heard about this Yes Day foolishness" she says, as she shakes her head with a smile.

"Okay, so let's set some ground rules," Mom starts. "First, you cannot ask for any purchases over $100, okay?"

"Okay."

"We cannot do anything illegal or dangerous."

"Got it."

"And we cannot go outside of the GTA."

"Okay, okay. Don't worry, Mom. I won't ask for anything crazy! It sounds like we're ready to get started, so my first request of the day is to have only bacon for breakfast!" I declare.

"Okay, sounds good," Mom chuckles. Grandma lets out an exasperated sigh and hands me my plate.

Yes Day starts out great. So far, I've been able to enjoy a protein-packed, but salty, bacon-only breakfast, followed by my choice of pyjamas as my outfit of the day. I then ask Mom to pick up Kara, to take us to the mall, so that we can buy some new fidget toys.

It's getting to lunchtime, which means that it's time for Kara and me to put our plan into action.

"Mom, Kara and I are starting to get hungry. Can we grab some lunch and have a picnic at the park by Grandma's house?" I ask.

"Sure, what would you like?"

"How about a family meal from the Portuguese chicken place?" Mom, Dad, and I always loved that Portuguese chicken, and especially the yummy pasteis de nata for dessert.

"Coming right up," Mom says. We stop at the Portuguese spot, pick up our food, and head to the park.

When we get to the park, Mom sees Dad's car right away. She parks and glares at me in the passenger seat. I try to avoid Mom's gaze by staring out the windshield. Meanwhile, I can hear Kara shifting around in the back seat, trying to figure out how to make herself invisible. Mom's eyes stay fixated on me.

"Cayden, is your dad going to be at this picnic?" she asks.

"Well…umm…yeah…" I finally look at her sheepishly. "But, Mom, you can't not go! This is still my Yes Day!"

"Okay, fine," she says, but I can see that she's not happy.

We get out of the car and walk toward Dad, who's sitting on a rock near the jungle gym, scrolling on his phone. He looks up, and I notice a little bit of shock on his face, seeing our guest of honour. I whip out the picnic blanket out of my backpack, and Kara takes the brown paper bag from Mom and starts laying out the meal.

"Hi, Asha," Dad says to Mom hesitantly. "It looks like we've been set up." He shifts his feet awkwardly.

"Yeah, I guess this is what happens when we let these young people participate in these social media challenges, eh? This is definitely the last time I sign up for any Yes Day!"

They share a nervous chuckle and join Kara and I on the ground: Mom, sitting on my right, and Dad to my left. Now seated, Dad pulls out his phone again, and Mom stares off into the distance. I look across at Kara, and she gives me the cringe face.

"I don't know what to say, Terrell," Mom says, after a few awkward minutes, "I guess we might as well enjoy this lovely spread?" She reaches for the roasted chicken, starts cutting it up, then shares food on our plates. Mom and Dad dig in.

"Soooo...how 'bout them Jays?" Dad offers, after a few more awkward minutes.

Kara and I look up hopeful, waiting for their eyes to lock, for a spark or even just a little twinkle in their eyes to be ignited, any sign of love.

"I don't really follow them anymore," Mom says, with a little bit of an attitude. "That was your thing."

Dad sighs deeply. After that, they barely look up from their plates.

I lean over to Mom and whisper in her ear: "Mom, can you be nice and just talk to Dad, please? As my final Yes Day request?"

Mom shakes her bowed head and responds under her breath: "I'm sorry, Cayden. This is one Yes Day request I don't think I can do right now."

I shift back to my spot and try to focus on the jungle gym in the distance, because I don't want her, Dad, or even Kara to see the hot tears that are beginning to well up in my eyes. To my dismay, we spend the rest of the meal in silence.

"Grandma, they're impossible! I couldn't even get them to have a proper conversation. And Kara and I made it so easy for them, too. All they had to do was talk to each other, like normal human beings! And then, on top of it, now I can't even post my challenge. Mom decided that she wasn't going to participate anymore!"

Grandma pours the last bit of tea from the teapot into my mug. It feels good to sit down and have her listen to my heart.

"Grandson, I know you're upset. But yuh know, yuh can lead a horse to water, but yuh cyaa make it drink," she says gently. Grandma was always good at coming up with some random West Indian proverbs.

"Ugh, Grandma, I don't get it," I say, looking at her quizzically.

"Cayden, the only person we can control on this earth is ourselves," she offers, matter-of-factly, as she clears the saucers from the table.

I go up to my room, thinking about what Grandma had said. I'm actually a little bit annoyed. Does she think that I'm trying to "control" my parents? I'm not trying to control them. They are controlling me. Forcing me to change my home and my friends just because they can't get along! And while they're at it, they are ruining my life! Mom always says that I'm the most important thing to both her and Dad. So, why am I not important enough for them to put aside how they feel and make it work for my sake? Don't they care about how I feel? I'm always thinking about how they feel. Well, I'm always thinking about how they feel... toward each other.

Ohhh, I think I get it now. I guess I had never stopped to think about how my parents are feeling for themselves. I want them to get back together so badly, to make me happy; but maybe getting back together would not make them feel good for their own sakes. So I guess I need to focus on controlling myself. I mean, I thought that I was already controlling myself enough by not screaming at both of my parents about how much I hate what's going on! But maybe what I really need to start doing is controlling my attitude about the situation.

The days are much hotter. School is out again, and sixth grade is around the corner. When we first got to Grandma's house a year ago, I thought we were staying for a week. I had no idea that a week would become a year. I had no idea that a year later, my parents would still be living apart.

I still don't know what made Mom leave or how much longer we'll be here. I don't know whether my parents will ever get back together, or get back to the point where they could even call each other "friends." What I do know is that I could get used to staying at Grandma's house. I could get used to being at a new school, having new friends, living in a new neighbourhood, and seeing Kara more often. I don't have to witness my parents fighting anymore. I hang my clothes in my new closet, nothing else. No more hiding on the floor, no more waiting for my parents to stop screaming at each other. And, above all, I can get used to the feeling of being at peace with my parents, with our new living situation. I wouldn't trade that feeling for anything.

Clarissa's Letter

by Gayle Gonsalves

'm going to see snow," I told my cousins.

"It's just like that white stuff in the freezer," Ginger said.

"You're so lucky, Clarissa!" Ashton, Ginger's brother, added.

We knew little about snow. Our only exposure was through pictures and television, yet we spent many long hours sitting amongst the red hibiscus on my grandmother's veranda, discussing how the most amazing experience in the world would be to touch it. I was leaving the following day to Canada where I'd see snow for the first time.

My mother and I lived with my grandmother in a green board house with a colourful garden, filled with lush bougainvillea and yellow bells. My cousins and I were always together, either playing at the beach or exploring the rolling hills that surrounded my grandmother's land.

At night, while my mother worked, my grandmother would tell me stories. I loved the lilting sound of her voice as it rose and fell with each word in her dulcet accent. As she became more engrossed in her storytelling, her dark, wavy hair would gently fall into her face and she'd quietly push the stray strands into her bun.

On my last afternoon on the island, my uncle drove my cousins and me to the beach. I sat quietly in the backseat of my uncle's car observing the brightly coloured homes with pretty gardens and the cows languidly walking on the road. Then I heard the sound of the waves and inhaled the refreshing sea breeze.

My cousins and I raced each other to the sea. This was our ritual. At age nine, I was the smallest and slowest, and always the last to jump into the water. Our laughter rose above the waves as we played tag. When our fingers became too wrinkled and cold, we ran to the shore and built a grand sandcastle, complete with a moat and drawbridge.

I was on the shore when my uncle yelled it was time to go. Without thinking, I ran back into the sea and splashed the water high into the air and it rained on me. I laughed as the cool cascading water hit my skin. I wanted to do this one last time before I left.

Back home, I dangled my feet over the gallery. Below me the ants prodded through the dirt. My cousins sat next to me. We were not speaking. They were upset because I kept boasting that I would see snow. They told me to stop talking, but I continued.

A car stopped in front of my grandmother's house. It was time to leave. I said bye to my cousins. They stared at me, eyes empty of emotion. My eyes pleaded with them but they walked away. My grandmother noticed the tension between my cousins and me and pulled me into her warm, comforting arms. Those arms held me at birth. I then realized I was also leaving her for another country. I felt a sudden fear for what was ahead and clung to her as we drove to the airport. She reassured me that the rift between my cousins and me would heal.

The loudspeaker announced our flight. I kissed my grandmother goodbye. She held me so hard it felt as if she would squeeze all the air out of me. For a moment, I wasn't sure I could leave her. My mother stood next to my grandmother, their bright dresses dancing in the breeze. I got tired of them staring at each other and tugged my mother's hand but she ignored me. Another announcement came over the speaker. My mother hugged my grandmother and then grabbed my hand. I scrambled to keep up with her. We sat in silence on the plane, arriving in Canada several hours later.

"Where's the snow?" I asked, surprised by the bright sun and warm air..

My mother saw my confused expression and said, "It's summer, Clarissa."

"Where did the snow go?"

"Don't worry, Clarissa, it'll snow, but first the weather has to change. It's hot now. When it gets cold, it will snow."

"But I have nothing to tell Ginger and Ashton."

"Clarissa, you're in a new country; there's lots to tell them before the snow comes."

Summer in Canada was filled with long days of bright sunlight—the sun was still shining when I went to bed. It annoyed me that the temperature was as hot as Antigua's because all I wanted to do was tell my cousins that I had seen snow.

The first few weeks in my new country were lonely. I spent a lot of time watching cartoons. I had no friends and we lived in a small apartment, with no backyard. I missed my grandmother. I missed swimming and playing at the beach. I missed my cousins.

Several weeks later, my mother started preparing me for winter with a new wardrobe. I now had furry boots that I could wear when it snowed. Each morning, I awoke with the expectation of snow but it didn't come. I could not write my cousins; there wasn't much to tell them because I had no friends and I was alone most of the time.

The temperature fell and it ushered in a new season. I was awed by the spectacular colours of that first autumn. The leaves turned fiery red and the earth became a magical golden carpet. My mother and I walked through parks and marvelled at the different colours. I wanted to tell my cousins about this beautiful season but couldn't. I felt a pang of sadness when I thought about how I had bragged about seeing snow and I didn't know how to say sorry.

The temperature continued to dip. One day I sighed and saw a white cloud hanging before me. Puzzled, I sighed again and another cloud formed. I sighed all day, fascinated by the tiny clouds I was creating. Despite all these changes, there was no snow and no news for my cousins. My grandmother wrote my mother and she filled me in with all the news. I wanted to write but it hadn't snowed. With each passing day, I felt even more ashamed that I had bragged that I'd see snow. I realized how much I missed my cousins and grandmother. I had no friends and often stared at the swings in the park wishing my cousins were here to play with me.

Then I awoke one November morning to a white sheet that covered everything. The incredible event had come! My mother joined me and we were silent with wonder. Everywhere was white—from the parking lot to the branches of trees to rooftops. Nothing was left untouched, as if we were in a new world, blanketed in smooth white frosting.

"It's so pretty," my mother said. "It doesn't look real. It's even prettier than in pictures."

"It's magical, Mommy! It's truly magic."

I put on the boots that had been waiting patiently for this moment and ran down the stairs. When I stepped outside, I was amazed at the stillness of the falling snow. Unlike rain, it fell quietly, disturbing no one, only changing the face of the earth. I stuck out my tongue to taste the snowflakes. To my surprise, it melted when it touched my tongue, and its coolness slid quietly down my throat.

The schoolyard was a frenzy of activity. Snowballs sailed menacingly through the air seeking targets. Some kids rolled larger balls to build snowmen, while those who weren't making snowballs slid down the hill, their laughter echoing through the schoolyard.

A girl from my class tapped my shoulder. She smiled mischievously and threw a snowball into my face. At first, I was stunned by its cold sting, but after my initial shock, I grabbed some snow, rolled it into a ball, and ran after her.

I arrived home later than usual after an afternoon playing in the snow and making new friends. I grabbed a pen and paper and began a letter to my cousins:

Dear Ginger and Ashton:

I'm so sorry that it took me so long to write to you. When I arrived in Canada, it was hot and there was no snow. I was also really lonely without you. I didn't do very much but I thought about you all the time. I wasn't very nice before I left because I boasted a lot about going away. I'm sorry and I promise never to do that again. I miss you so much.

Today it snowed and I really wish that you were here with me so that we could play in it together. There was lots of snow and it was more beautiful than any picture. Snow is light but cold. When you hold it in your bare hands, it melts quickly. There is so much you can do with the snow. You can make snowballs and snowmen. You can even build a snow castle—kind of like the sandcastles we built at the beach.

You won't believe it, but I made gigantic snowballs, bigger than a beach ball, by rolling and rolling the snow. That's how you make snowmen. Some kids lay down in it and made angels by flapping their arms. That was so neat to see!

I miss you so much and want to hear from you. Forgive me, and write soon.

Love, Clarissa.

Authors

Jaimie Franchi is a writer, English instructor, and gardener. Her work for children has been supported by grants from the Canada Council for the Arts, CBC/Radio-Canada, and the Conseil des arts et des lettres du Québec. Her writing for adults has appeared in *filling Station*, *Poems for the Solstice*, *Kitchen Table Magazine*, *Farmerish*, and *Athens Free Press*. She holds an MA in Literature from the University of Georgia.

Caroline Bennett is a former teacher and librarian with experience in the UK, Hawai'i, and Canada. She holds degrees in Education, English Literature, and Educational Foundations. Caroline writes picture books and short stories, and was longlisted for the CANSCAIP Writing for Children competition in 2020. She blends her commitment to education with a passion for storytelling, aiming to inspire curiosity and a lifelong love of reading. Caroline lives in Toronto with her three children.

Latoya Belfon is an author and storyteller who brings meaningful ideas to life through engaging, impactful books. As the founder of Labworks Publishing, she supports writers in finding their voice and publishing with purpose. Her work blends creativity with thoughtful messaging, focusing on stories that resonate across audiences. With a passion for diverse perspectives and transformative narratives, Latoya writes to inspire reflection, build connection, and highlight the power of words.

Deborah Ross-Attas is an award-winning educator and children's writer based in Toronto. Inspired by her three sons' childhood adventures, she weaves curiosity and humor into her stories. Deb coordinates and volunteers with Booster Reading, a literacy program, and enjoys time with her four grandchildren and three granddogs. When not teaching or writing, she takes art lessons, goes on long walks, and dances her heart out in Dancefit classes.

Julianne Mundle is the author of *Come with the Fire*. She was featured in the Writers' Collective of Canada's 2022 anthology series *Front Lines: Resilience—I open my Mouth to Speak.* Born in Jamaica, Julianne now lives in Mississauga, Ontario. She holds a BA from McMaster University and a Post-Graduate Certificate in Creative Writing from Humber College. She is currently an MBA student at Smith School of Business, Queen's University.

Peter Tetteh Loveson is a Ghanaian poet and creative fiction writer. His work, influenced by his travels and life experiences, explores themes of connection, hope, grief, and the human condition. Known for his evocative language, Peter captures quiet moments and everyday wisdom. Outside of writing, he enjoys spending time with family and friends, playing music, capturing the world through photography, and supporting local cafes.

Saira Batasar-Johnie identifies as a brown, Indo-Caribbean Canadian. She is an author, Child and Youth Care Practitioner, and Registered Social Worker, passionate about sharing the history and practices of Indo-Caribbean people. Through her words, Saira aims to educate and inspire. Her book *Dear Divya* seeks to encourage young people on their journey of self-discovery.

Abigail Grimes is a Canadian, multi-genre author based in rural Ontario and working in Toronto. She draws inspiration from the diverse environments around her. Abigail has been featured at the Salon of the Refused, BlackLit Durham, and the Northumberland Festival of the Arts. She is a member of the Writers' Community of Durham Region.

Ndija Anderson-Yantha is a second-generation Caribbean Canadian author, lawyer, speaker, and university administrator, passionate about EDI, literacy, and combating anti-Black racism. Her debut book, *What Are You Gonna Do with that Hair?*, celebrates Black hairstyles. A graduate of Spelman College (BA, political science, French) and McGill University (LLB, BCL), Ndija is also a former Thomas J. Watson Fellow. She lives in the Greater Toronto Area.

Gayle Gonsalves' short stories have appeared in *The Bluelight Corner, In the Black, The Black Notes, Tongues of the Ocean*, and *So the Nailhead Bend, So the Story Ends*. Her first book, *Painting Pictures and Other Stories*, was published in 2013. Her debut novel, *My Stories Have No Endings*, received six Indie Awards. Gonsalves is a graduate of York University and lives in Toronto, where she continues to write.

Editor & Illustrator

Juleus Ghunta is a Chevening Scholar, poet, and literacy advocate. He has authored and edited several books, and his poems and essays have appeared in more than thirty journals. A recipient of multiple awards, including the Charles Causley Trust Poetry Prize and Poetry Archive Wordview Prize, his journey overcoming adversity has been featured by the BBC, CBC, NPR, and in *Trauma Proof*, a book by Benjamin Perks, Head of Campaigns and Advocacy at UNICEF HQ.

Anil N. Singh is an art director, designer, and illustrator based in Toronto. A firm believer in imagination and hard work, he dedicates his time to creative projects and design. When he's not working, Anil can be found teaching or practicing Bikram yoga, enjoying delicious food, or drawing letters.